T0207804

TWELVE YEARS
DOWN THE ROAD

TWELVE YEARS
DOWN THE ROAD

ALAN NEIL

 iUniverse®

TWELVE YEARS DOWN THE ROAD

iUniverse books may be ordered through booksellers or by contacting:

iUniverse
1663 Liberty Drive
Bloomington, IN 47403
www.iuniverse.com
1-800-Authors (1-800-288-4677)

Because of the dynamic nature of the Internet, any web addresses or links contained in this book may have changed since publication and may no longer be valid. The views expressed in this work are solely those of the author and do not necessarily reflect the views of the publisher, and the publisher hereby disclaims any responsibility for them.

Any people depicted in stock imagery provided by Thinkstock are models, and such images are being used for illustrative purposes only. Certain stock imagery © Thinkstock.

ISBN: 978-1-5320-2417-7 (sc)
ISBN: 978-1-5320-2418-4 (e)

Library of Congress Control Number: 2017908046

Print information available on the last page.

iUniverse rev. date: 05/22/2017

CONTENTS

CHAPTER 1

THE MAGIC OF TV

Joe, Al and Fred were at the tinder ages of 13, 11, and 9. They lived in the country and the wild life management next to their Dads farm was their play ground but schooling and church had them mixing with other kids who were not their cousins. It was a strange and different world. Other kids seemed to think their homes were their castles but the boys knew the forest was their kingdom. They all could shoot rifles and shotguns and the animals in the woods respected them. At school they saw other kids going thru childhood diseases and they didn't fear the diseases but felt sorry for the kids who had them. Having the mumps was their biggest fear and not because of the associated swelling in their throat and ears but it was rumored that when you had the mumps your testicles would also swell so big that they couldn't walk. On some Saturday nights they would all get into their Dad's 1948 Dodge to drive into the nearest town which was more than 20 miles away. Mostly they would drive down the main street looking at other people driving up and down Main Street but as a reward to the boys for not talking too much, their Dad would stop at the Tasty Freeze drive in to order soft ice cream. A hot Texas night was made for soft swirled ice cream and the girls working as car hops seemed to have the best job in town as they took their orders, delivered the ice cream and Daddy paid them with a smile as mother closely watched his behavior. Joe would always finish eating his ice cream cone first, Fred would eat slower and would never finish his cone before it melted over hi and the car seat and Al would eat slowly in fear of the dreaded brain freeze which seemed to be a punishment for eating too fast. When the ice cream treat was finished they would drive back down to the Good Year tire store to see the new invention of television. The tire store had a couple of the new invention sat up in the windows of the store and even though the store closed at five PM people would park in front of the store to watch the televisions. The sounds were impossible but on Saturday they would be showing Houston Wrestling. The boys would get out of the car and sit as close to the store windows as possible completely amazed how the television could transmit live pictures from Houston which was 120 miles away. Mother would tell them to not get too close to the windows as the dreaded fear or radiation poisoning was her concern and perhaps blindness caused by it. The boys were more interested in the wrestling moves as the wrestlers slammed each other into submission. They wanted a TV in their home and as soon as they drove home the started questioning their parents about how they could get a TV. The cost was almost 200 dollars and Dad only made 25 dollars a week. It seemed impossible but they would find a way because it became their obsession and the dream of owning a TV would not go away. Finally after weeks of questioning about how they would get a TV Dad came up with a plan. During this time of questioning the boys sat in the church where mother's uncle was the preacher. They rarely listened to his preaching's but when he preached that the TV was the devils work shop and people would go to hell for watching TV. They feared for their lives as they listened but still they wanted a TV in their home and it seemed each time they went to church the preacher said that anyone could go to hell for almost any thing. On one occasion Dad said that the preacher would likely be the first one to go to hell for drinking and chasing women. The preacher once said that he became a preacher because he had been so worthless that only God could save him. Al wondered where the preacher got his money from because he and his family seemed to be the best dressed people in the church. Most everyone else in the church wore clothes that were made from pastel printed cotton made from old dairy sack feed bags. Dad told him that the money collected during the service went to the preacher and he didn't have to work like everyone else. Mother offered no advice because the preacher was her uncle. The boys were not afraid to go to hell for watching a TV that showed the Houston wrestling and the Nashville Grand Ole Opera. They wanted a TV. Finally daddy explained his plan to the boys and as with most of his plans they included a lot of work and a lot of time. The price of a TV and the price of a bale of cotton were compared and after expenses they were about the same price. The boys had to become farmers and grow cotton to earn money for the TV. Dad explained that a bale of cotton sold for about one dollar a pound and a bale of cotton usually weighed close to 500 pounds. That didn't mean they would earn 500 dollars because they had expenses to produce the cotton. They had to prepare the field, buy the seeds and pay to get the owner of the tractor and plowing equipment. They would hire their cousin to plow the field and pay him when they sold the cotton. He said he wasn't sure about the prices but they could earn 300 dollars if all went well and the bugs didn't destroy the cotton plants. Dad said they couldn't afford to buy fertilizer and bug spray so they would need to plant 5 acres and check for bugs daily. The boys had a plan to get a TV; The TV that would connect them to the world. They got excited and started planning. A couple of years earlier they had gotten in trouble with the radio and the memories were still fresh. The radio sat on top of the ice box. The ice box looked like a refrigerator but inside it only had a fan and once a week Dad put in a block of ice to keep things inside from spoiling and to provide ice for use in drinking tea or cool aid. One Saturday night the boys stayed home while Mom and Dad went next door to visit with the neighbors. Joe wanted to listen to the radio show named the Shadow. The imagination of 3 boys aged 4, 6 and 10 came to life. Joe tuned in the radio and the weird voice scared Fred. He started telling Joe to turn it off. Joe refused so Fred stood up on the 5 gallon can of lard that mother used for cooking to reach the radio and turn it off. Then the lid of the can came off and one of his legs went to the bottom of the can of grease. Alan and Joe pulled him out and his leg was coated with lard. He wasn't much taller than the can so his short pants were completely covered with lard. Quickly they got his new pants, helped him scrape off the lard and hid the greased up pants for hiding and washing. The plan went well except they forgot that when they pulled him out one of his shoes stayed in the lard. Next day while mom was cooking she noticed a hole in the lard; she got a long fork and fished out Fred's shoe. The boys were punished to lying even they didn't tell anyone anything except during interrogation they told that the radio had scared Fred. Didn't seem to matter their intentions were honorable and they were punished. They would have to be careful with the TV.

The plan started in the spring after Dad taught them to read the Farmers Almanac to know when to plant for best results. Joe had done a visual survey of the slope of the land and they started working on proper drainage in case of too much rain. Al envisioned the length and width of the rows for planting and how they would curve for natural drainage. When their cousin started plowing the field they told him exactly what they wanted and with a big smile he followed their instructions. When the rows were ready for planting they took a stick and punched holes in the ground and put 3 cotton seeds in each hole making sure the spaces between each hole was exactly the right distance. They checked each day for the seeds to sprout out of the ground and start growing. Bugs be dammed, no bugs were going to eat their TV. Chopping out the weeds that sprouted along with the cotton plants became a chore. It was a lot of work and no excuses were acceptable. It seemed that spring quickly became summer and summer quickly became autumn as their watched the cotton grow from sprouts to growing the cotton bole until the entire plant turned brown and the bole opened to show cotton. Then after being told to wait a little longer they started picking cotton. Each day after school they picked cotton, weighed cotton and put it in a cotton trailer. They all had cuts on their fingers from the prickly dried cotton boles. Finally the cotton was picked and on the twenty mile trip to the cotton gin the boys rode in the trailer on top of the cotton waving to all passers by. They watched the vacuum hose suck each piece of cotton into the cotton gin. As soon as the last piece of cotton was fed into the cotton gin the boys demanded their money. Daddy told them that the gin did not buy the cotton they only took out the seeds and bailed it. They were silent during the gin work and looked own with pride as their bale of cotton came out of the gin with a label telling who the owner was. Daddy told them that the bale weighed more than 500 pounds and they would get their money next week after a cotton buyer had purchased it. They were quiet on the ride home thinking about what could possibly go wrong during the next week. It would be a long week but they were rewarded when they went to the gin to get their money. The money was only a piece of paper and this was another disappointment but daddy explained that he would go to the bank, cash the check and they could get their money to buy the TV. They must wait another week and it seemed like an eternity. After the check was cashed Daddy paid the cousin for all the tractor work. The check was for more than five hundred dollars. The tractor work cost almost two hundred but they still had more than enough to buy the TV. The following week they went inside the Goodyear store and picked out the TV from one of the three available. The cost was more than 200 dollars because they also needed a 60 foot antenna to receive the picture. The antenna came with a motor mount so the signal could be aligned with the antenna. They listened as the salesman explained that there were only two stations and one was in Houston and one was in Galveston. You had to rotate the antenna when you changed stations. The TV was an 18 inch Motorola with a silver screen that could show only black and white. The boys didn't listen as the salesman show them the 3 knobs that controlled vertical and horizontal movement and the contrast. They thought that only

3 switches could not be so complicated. Then they learned that the antenna must be installed by a professional installer. Their order was added to the work schedule and now had to wait another week for it to be installed. They were afraid to tell anyone they were getting a TV and the again listened to the preacher's sermon about the TV being the devils workshop. Finally the installation was completed and everyone knew they had a TV because the old farm house now had a 60 foot antenna beside it. All the kids on the school bus told all the kids at school that they had a TV. Mother insisted that the extra money from the cotton was spent buying new school clothes and shoes for the upcoming winter. Almost a year had passed since daddy told them how to get a TV. He seemed proud of the boys and except for Saturday nights he let them choose what to watch. They quickly got in tune with the world. So many cowboy shows, a puppet named Howdy Doody with a clown named Claribell and a show called the Mickey Mouse Club. They watched and learned. Mother even watched during the day; some soap operas that never seemed to have an ending story. Some boxing, some wrestling and always some new ideas every day came from the TV. It took a few years for the new to wear off and it ended abruptly when daddy thought that the boys were becoming addicted to watching the TV and he bought 200 head of goats for the boys to take care of. In a couple of years they had to take care of more than 500 goats. The preacher may have been right because the TV story did not end well thanks to the goats but their dreams of being cowboys lived on. Fred got to live his dream of being a cowboy and even became a professional bull rider. Joe and Al became soldiers.

CHAPTER 2

1700 THE HOMELESS PEOPLE

To view Scotland from the air at low altitude on a clear day tells the beginning of a long story of peoples struggles. The clear signs of wind and cold combined with crashing cold sea water onto heaps of rocks make it seem impossible for people to live there but somehow this part of the world would produce some of the best frontiersmen and some of the best soldiers the world has ever seen. They would make trips that other people couldn't make. They would survive in all conditions and even prosper. They would find the trails into the heart of America and they would they would never bow to any King or man. The stories in this book are about some of those people. The kind of people that have never held a bag pipe but still cry when they hear one played.

The Kings of England had lost fear of the Scotts, their Viking friends with their continuous history of trouble making. He had taken the Scotts land, replacing most of them with Anglo Saxons and moved them to farms in the strange country of Ireland. Hundreds of years after the Britt's forced transmigration they would slowly remake the entire British culture into the same culture the Scotts had before they were forced off their land. Even the British royalty would wear Kilts and the sound of bagpipes would be what England listened to as they marched into war. The great transmigration had begun.

The first Scotts that first came to America were a people dying of starving because of no hunting lands, over taxation and poor crops. These people found their way to the Americas. Daniel had been one of these:

The weather had been worse than usual and surviving had been difficult. Daniels parents had died mostly of starvation but also from despair. He had lived with family members after his parents had died and then he found his way around the city of Oban trying to find enough work to survive. He had no skills to market, slept on the streets and took only day labor jobs for his meager earnings. That all changed the day he met the most beautiful girl he had ever seen. Her name was Sara and she had come with her family from a small Island of Jara off the coast of Scotland. They were in town to sell their whiskey. Her family was also poor and the bad weather on the Island made life hard but they knew how to make a very good whiskey and that was their only source of cash.

The love affair was fast and furious and it would carry Daniel home with Sara. It seemed that even getting to Sara's Island home was dangerous and the dangers of sea whirlpools kept away most of the bad guys and tax collectors. The Island was small and held no military importance except for Viking ports. Most Scotts and Britt's ignored the Island because sailing to it was dangerous. Daniel was taken into Sara's clan but the family had become too big and most of the Island's sparse food wasn't enough to sustain them. The deer that had fed them for years was in short supply. Domesticated animals didn't fare well on the Island because of the conditions of nature and the dreaded tax men in Oban had learned to tax their whiskey at the place it was sold. They knew secretes for making good whiskey and good whiskey always commanded a premium price. The spring water and the peat for cooking were special and it showed up in quality when they made their whiskey. The new laws for taxing whiskey were a different matter and the local government in Oban wanted to monopolize and control the whiskey. Some whiskey makers ended up in jail and being in jail would steal there honor, no one wanted to end up in jail. Some of the small whiskey makers sold their whiskey to cooperatives that blended it together for export. It seemed impossible to continue making and selling whiskey for enough profit to feed the clan

James was the oldest of the Bouie family and he had heard of America. The land had more deer than any family could eat; the land so rich that anything could be grown and there were no enforceable laws about making whiskey in the new country. He saved enough for ship fare, packed his family and came to America. The family arrived in Charlestown, South Carolina and discovered that owning land was hard but there was really no need to own land because it seemed to be an endless supply of it if you just kept moving west. Generations of Daniels and Saras moved west. Moving West was not without dangers but the generations learned to kill animals and eat bears and live among the Indians. Nothing seemed seem to stop them from continually moving West. They moved across Georgia to Alabama and then on to Mississippi. They settled in camps until the years of moving had passed and then clan leader James Bouie decided he was too old to move. They built a town, made large cotton farms and bought some slaves to help run the farm. Their slaves were provided with education, a place to worship and they shared their lives with their slaves. The 4th generation of Daniel & Sara was now almost fifty years old and most generations had twelve children. Some were born in Mississippi and some in Alabama.

Daniel the fourth didn't agree with owning slaves and he decided to move his family across the river into Arkansas. In 1750 there were few people of European descent in Arkansas. The two oldest sons had married girls from the Gilmore family while they were in Alabama. The family would cross the Mississippi south of Memphis and move to the part of Arkansas where the great piney wood forest starts. Woods for hunting and river delta for farming would provide all their needs. The family would produce not only crops and food for the family; but they also produced soldiers for the American Revolution and each war that followed. The American civil war would find family members serving the Blue and the Gray. When the war was over they all came home to the same home. None of the immediate family owned slaves before the war and they all served in the military. Which side didn't seem to matter because none of them were politically inclined? The unofficial family mottos were "Never work for the Government, any government" and always serve in the military.

The women were famous for their beauty and they kept the family together and the men under control by teaching them to read and write and reading to them the Bible. They did not preach to each other, worshiped only in their homes or at community camp meetings, paid their fair taxes, continued to make whiskey for sale and did not understand they were poor. Family honor was so deep that they were forbidden to speak ill of others and they were all taught that it was not because the others were either good or bad but speaking ill of others was something only bad people did. Expressing to the public the judgment of anything outside the home or family was forbidden.

It seemed so unfortunate that all the boys loved to fight and would never pass up the opportunity. The skill of fighting was developed early and the skill of survival was also developed early. Up until the boys were old enough to work with the men they spent their time in the woods exploring. All the boys had knives before they were four years old and learned to shoot a gun shortly there after. Any six year old boy shooting a twelve gauge shotgun will quickly learn respect for both the gun and what he was shooting at. A simple rule of being forced to eat whatever you killed makes gun control simple.

One day the sons, Archie and Daniel the fifth, were walking home and they met a stranger who was also a drunken man. They were in their early teens and the drunk amused himself by making them dance by shooting at their feet. They went home got their squirrel guns and went back to find the drunk. The drunken man was upset when they confronted him and he was shot to death after refusing to give them an apology. They went home and told their parents what had happened. The family talked to the sheriff and he informed them that the boys must be tried for the killing but he would tell no one for three days. They left for Texas that night. The two teenagers would live off the land, follow the off beat trails and river bottoms until they found a safe place to live in Texas. They eventually settled in the Neches river bottom just outside an Indian reservation. It had taken the family just over 150 years to produce their first Texans. Their Bouie cousins in Mississippi had produced their first Texan a generation earlier. They settled down where the trees stop growing and the prairies start. Years later it would be proclaimed a National Forrest and except for a few homesteads the area they live in would become a Wild Life Refuge. Their spirit still lives in those woods. Archie would take a wife from the local Indian tribe who was being pushed out by the Cherokee and Alabama Indians and start a family. Daniel would join the Army when he was nineteen years old. Serve in WWI and die on the battle fields in France. Archie would father and raise 3 sons and 2 daughters. Edward was the youngest and last son. He would father and raise 3 sons. Al was the second son of Edward. The two daughters would raise twelve children and all the sons would become bankers. They would become the only family in the county to employ English butlers. Al's father and his uncles would all become working ranchers. Al's brothers would become military or law enforcement.

CHAPTER 3

1946 UNCLE BUCK COMES HOME

Al was almost four years old when Uncle Buck came home from the War. A few months earlier his father came home from the war and he could remember this strange man holding him and smiling at him and his brothers. His youngest brother was almost two years old and had just started to walk. His father loved to hold him, Al and his older brother. He just held them saying nothing, he had not been there for the birth of the youngest boy and the youngest looked exactly like him. He had a full head of black hair and deep, dark brown eyes. Al's father just held his three sons on his lap and smiled. He walked with a limp and needed to rest often. His grandmother cooked sweet potatoes for him in her old wood stove and he shared with them. Al was amazed at his father drinking coffee and eating sweet potatoes. When ever grandmother cooked sweet potatoes Al and his older brother usually got in trouble for swiping a few and eating them under the house while they played. Sweet potatoes were the favorite dessert in the family and coffee was available for adult drinking all day long, no child was allowed to drink coffee. Occasionally Al's older brother was given a cup of warm milk which he pretended was coffee and would drink it from a saucer like his grandfather did. Al noticed that his grandfather seemed to be a lot busier after his father came home and spent most of his days in the field working. Al and his brothers spent most of their time playing under the old farm house using his grandmothers snuff bottles for cars. The house was a full four feet above the ground and it was cool under the house. The loose sand offered good entertainment for the boys. They didn't have to worry about getting clothes dirty because all they wore was a pair of short pants. When the snuff bottle cars became a bore they would spend time catching doodle bugs. Doodle bugs were some small ugly caterpillar looking bugs that would burrow down in the sand leaving only a small hole for air. They had learned that to catch a doodle bug they must spit on a broom straw, make a small mud ball of spit and sand and gently put the wet straw down the hole. Al grandfather had taught them that they must say "doodle bug, doodle bug come out of your hole, your house is on fire, the coffee will boil over and your children will burn" they learned that the doodle bug would start eating the wet saliva mud and would hold on as you pulled the straw from the hole. It was like craw fishing. They would put their doodle bugs in a small glass jar to show every one how many bugs they had caught. Al's father seemed to delight in seeing his boys catch doodle bugs and Al's older brother would always become excited when he caught one. He would point out that his bug had different colors and was larger. Al's younger brother would mostly just watch Al.

Their Mothers family lived on the next farm over and they had spent most of their time with their mother's parents while their father had been off to war. They were not allowed to play under their house because it was too low and there was no sand to play in, so they spend many hours playing in the old barn. The corn crib usually was good for seeing and catching rats and an occasional snake but mostly while in the barn the boys and their cousins played war. The barnyard was usually full of corn cobs and this was their weapons. They would chose sides and the battle would begin. The game ended when the next to last boy had been hit with a corn cob. Al never won the war but he had learned that a wet corn cob full of mud left a lasting impression on the person you hit with it. Al's older brother always won the war game but they had fun hiding from each other and then a surprise hit taking the person out of the game. It seemed that all the uncles and cousins were away fighting in the real war and each Saturday night the family gathered in the living room around the old battery radio to hear the news of the war. The children had to be still and be quiet or risk a knot on the head. The children had no idea what the radio said but they listened and waited for the news to turn to the Louisiana Hayride music or the Grand Old opera. The radio station seemed to drift in and out and no one touched the dial except grandpa. One night came the news "they war is over and the boys are coming home". Grandpas seemed to just become fully relaxed and the grandmothers cried. Uncle Buck was finally coming home. Al's father smiled a full smile; his best friend was coming home. Mother seemed so happy her brother had made it through the war. Most of the other boys in the area had come home in boxes with flags over the coffins. These boys had come home in coffins that were never opened before they were buried. Uncle Buck was alive and he was coming home.

The mail box was half a mile from the house and no one knew who was bringing Uncle Buck home but they all knew he would arrive at the mail box first; so Al and his brother waited at the mail box. The mailman came in his black ford coupe and out of the back seat sprang Uncle Buck. He was a strange sight in his Blue navy uniform with the long collar and saucer looking hat. Even his shoes looked strange, they seemed to have a whole can of polish on them and even in the dust you could see your face from the top of his shoes. The boys watched as he pulled out his bag and ask who they were. Al's older brother told him their names and he hugged them, picking them both up at one time and gave them a big smile. They all walked towards the farm house. When the boys asked him where he had been he told them a lot of places. He mentioned Borneo, the Philippians, New Guinea and Guadalcanal and Japan, he said he had been all over the world but neither of the boys recognized any of the names. On the way to the house he stopped and looked every where. At first he looked at the fields and the crops, then he looked at the woods and finally he looked to the sky but while he looked at the sky he closed his eyes and Al noticed a tear running down his dark sun tanned face. He caught Al looking at his tear and he said "It's been a long time since I last saw this place, looks like they have painted the barn." Grandpa believed all barns should be painted red.

When they arrived at the house the entire family was standing on the front porch and as soon as grandma saw him she came running towards him so fast that Al could believe it. How could grandma move so fast and scream so loud. After grandma turned him loose he hugged all the women, then he shook hands with all the men while grandpa stood at the end of the porch and watched. When he shook grandpa's hand grandpa wrapped his big arms around and hugged him like a bear. He told him that he was so happy he was home and the war was over. After grandpa got through hugging him every one went into the dining room for cake and coffee. Uncle Buck told them how he got back from San Diego. He traveled by train, bus, another bus, and then bumming a ride with the postman. Then he opened his bag and gave his mother a present, a small jade necklace which she would forever treasure, he handed grandpa a Japanese bayonet, no one else expected or got a present. At last he opened up a small sack that looked very oily. He poured the contents out on the dining room table. No one said anything but when someone asked him what they were looking at he said "Japanese ears" with a large smile. Grandma screamed and told him to get those ears out of the house and go bury them. The family looked in shock except Al's father. He just nodded his head and smiled.

Uncle Buck picked up the ears and went outside; Al followed and told him he would get a shovel. Uncle Buck said no he would dig a hole with his knife. The Navy uniform didn't look like it had a place for a knife because it didn't have any pockets but with one smooth motion he pulled a knife from inside his pants, opening it by bumping it on his thigh while lightly flicking his wrist. Uncle

Buck's knife looked clean and razor sharp. He dug a hole with the knife about a foot deep and placed the ears in the hole. Both Al and Uncle Buck knew the cats and chickens would dig up the ears but Uncle Buck didn't seem to care. He started crying again and his tears were not just a few. As tears ran down his face Al sat in his Lap and listened while he told him that if the family had seen the death of friends like he had they would understand. He said he would never forget his friends who died or the people who killed them. Most of his friends had been burned alive before their ship sank and many more had died waiting to be rescued from the water. He would never forget. At that moment Uncle Buck and Al bonded for life. Uncle Buck moved to Houston to raise his family and would always be a fireman. He ran the training academy in Houston and for over thirty years anyone wanting to be a fireman for the City of Houston must get approval from Uncle Buck. Al knew what his standards for becoming a fireman were. Simply put he sorted out men who would risk their own life to save a life. Years later Al would visit the places Uncle Buck had talked about that day and he would remember the pictures Uncle Buck had painted in his brain. The beaches of Guadalcanal looked so peaceful; the jungles of Borneo looked so hostile, the caves of New Guinea so serene, the cliffs of Okinawa so protective but Al knew they all had lots of American and Japanese blood on them. That sack of ears came from these places; maybe Al's presence brought the ears home.

CHAPTER 4

1962 DREAMS DON'T DIE

Al was a senior in high school. He was pretty much a loner except for a few close friends and his younger brother Fred. Fred was not a loner; he was active at several levels of school activity and very handsome. Al had played football but had absolutely no interest in the game. His only fun in football was blocking. He loved the hand to hand combat and took pride in knocking the on rushing defensive lineman backwards. Al absolutely loved the trap play where he would take a step back turn left behind the scrimmage line and lead the halfback around the corner and down field. He looked for a linebacker or corner back to wipe out, run over and humiliate. He could care less about the advance of the half back or how hard he got hit. Finally it seemed that football wasn't much fun because Al's real love was baseball. Throwing the ball a little faster, hitting the ball a little harder and further and catching everything hit at him. Al quit sports and thought only about his future. There seemed so many things he wanted to do but he could not see down the road far enough to know where it would take him. It was during the time he was in thinking about where to go and what to do that he became changed forever.

Fred had asked Al if he wanted to go to the Freshman Prom. Al knew his brother wanted to go and at first thought he needed Al's protection. It seemed that Fred was always in borderline trouble with older boys because of their girlfriends. Fred seemed to be a magnet for girls, they found him and he enjoyed being found. This wasn't the case. Fred went with his old girlfriend and another couple joined. Fred's girlfriend was named Ann and she asked Al if he minded stopping to pick up a friend of hers. The girl they picked up was a surprise. The 1951 brown Ford was packed and the AM radio blaring Buddy Holley as they stopped to pick up Ann's friend She set in the front seat next to Al but after saying "Hi" she turned away to talk to her friends in the back seat. She whispered an apologized for the smell that no one seemed to notice and said that she had used Purex to clean her coat. Al noticed that her coat was a cheap vinyl, much like the seat covers of Al's car. When she looked back at Al he noticed her eyes and face. She was petite with blond hair and eyes so green and shinny they would make emeralds look cheap. Al started to listen as this girl spoke. At first he had thought that Ann was fixing him up with one of her friends but this wasn't the case. As they drove to the dance she seemed so full of life and so happy that Al started to enjoy her presence.

When they arrived at the gym for the dance Al proceeded to distance himself from his brother and his friends. Al sat and watched until she saw him and insisted that he dance with her. Al didn't like dancing and didn't dance well or often but he relented and they danced: did they dance. Fast songs, slow songs they danced every song. The fast songs were two people showing each other some moves and then the other doing the moves. The slow songs were two bodies moving as one. Two strangers exploring touch, smell and moving in unison. It seemed to Al that her entire persona was something direct from Heaven. The scent of her hair, the warmth of her breath, the softness of her body and above that she seemed to be perfectly in tune with Al's every movement and thought. They were alone in the midst of a hundred other people. When the dance was over Al knew he was with someone special. On the way home they drove to a nearby lake at the insistence of Fred and Ann. When they parked so the other couples could make out it seemed his brother

Fred and Ann wanted to walk around the lake. Al stayed in the car with his new friend and continued their conversations about what's down the road and listened to the radio. Then they kissed. It was the first kiss Al had felt to his soul. Her kisses were soft moist and sweet. Al was in love and she was in love with him. No dreaming, no talking just soft sweet kisses that rocked their souls. It was if he had been waiting for that kiss his entire life

When they stopped at her house the lights were still on and Al walked her to the door. She opened the door and her father was sitting in the living room dressed in a pair of overalls with no shirt. He was a burley, hairy man and Al offered no conversation. He simply said good night and left. The universe was still spinning and he could still taste her kisses but Al's own green eyes were still glossed by the memory of hers. He was changed forever and knew what love meant, he loved everything about her.

The next week Al stopped driving to school, quit all after school activities so he could ride the same school bus that she rode. It didn't matter that he had to walk more than a mile from where the bus dropped him off and picked him up. He wanted to spend every minute possible with her. This mysterious Angel had lit his candle. He had never known anyone like her. She had told Al that her father would not let her go on dates nor stay overnight with friends. She was the oldest of five children and her mother was always sick. Her father was employed at a sawmill and this was her family's first year in town. They came from another sawmill town about an hours drive to the East. Her family was very religious and in case Al hadn't noticed she was not allowed to wear make up. Al had not noticed she didn't wear make up but he had memorized every feature of her face and body. She was blond with light freckles on her face and her eyes seemed to turn greener towards the outer edges and the white of her eyes was perfectly white. The fingernails showed signs of work and dishwashing and her skin seemed like milk but "no" Al had not notice she didn't wear make up.

Al's senior year was spent around her as much as possible. They managed one semi date. They met at the local movie theater to see Summer Place. They held hands for the entire movie but left the theater separately. The next week on the school bus they talked of a better life, she shared his dream of a better life but neither of them knew how to get one. After graduation Al left home to find work and education with a promise to return. He returned a year later and learned that her family had moved back to their hometown. Al also learned that she had broken her leg in a car accident. The broken leg never healed and her leg was removed. Al also learned that she lived only a few weeks after her leg had been amputated.

Al had not resolved his one night with an Angel. He had been in four wars and every time death seemed eminent he thought of her. When Al rode his dirt bike over the sand dunes of Arabia not knowing when he would fall into a subka and disappear forever as he reached speeds more than 100mph and he thought of how the bike responded to each of his body moves just like she did, he thought of her as he rode his bike alone and sometimes only in pale moon light. When Al drove alone through the jungles of Indonesia he thought of her. When Al battled lung cancer and its reoccurrence he thought of her. He laughed when he thought of all the people who were afraid to follow him or her to the other side but he always felt sorry for all who had never danced with an Angel. The strangest part about her was he could never say her name or mention his feelings for her to anyone. He often wondered how happy he would have been spending his entire life with her and he always concluded that some dreams just don't die. He did spend his entire life with her.

CHAPTER 5

1964 EQUALITY

A l had just finished high school and no interest in going off to college. He had no interest in anything except making money. In East Texas money was scarce and even though he had worked a job while attending high school the money was small and didn't seem to last. The best part of his high school job was delivering the Dallas Morning news. He would wake up at 3:00 am, drive to the bus station pick up a shipment of papers hot off the press, drive around town in the shortest fashion and throw the papers on the subscriber's lawn or place of their choice after he had rolled the paper in a log and tied it with twine string. Rainey days required it placed in the plastic bags sent down from Dallas. He always thought that the hours between 3 and 7 were the best hours of the entire day.

The 4 am crowd at the bus station was always the same type of people and it seemed unadvisable to befriend any of them except to give them free newspapers if Dallas had sent too many. You could see all the towns late night people and Al discovered that most of the late night people were either extremely lonely or up to no good. You could also see the early risers who couldn't wait to start another day. You could see the ladies of the night and all her friends but you also could see the drunks who wanted to get home before daylight and the politicians who wanted to get out of the neighborhood before the sun had risen. Al lived in a working class neighborhood but his paper route carried him to all parts of the town. Al never tired of seeing a house that the great Frank Lloyd Wright had designed, a home there that had a small creek running under the home. The factory owners were the wealthy and their houses were large colonial style that had a lot of land, dark windows and few neighbors. Most of the middle class lived in their brick ranch styles with cars parked in the street. Al's favorite customers were the Brooks brother's food warehouse and main headquarters. They were located only two blocks from the bus station and they bought 5 newspapers each day. The drop place for the papers was on the loading dock. This bunch was a grocery supplier to almost all of the food stories for 30 miles in each direction. They were probably the only ones who knew who Neil was because the company was owned and operated by five brothers and Neil's cousin had came home from the Korean was a hero and he had married the only daughter and sole survivor of their empire. All the five brothers had produced only one child.

Collection days were usually horrible for Al but especially bad at the Brooks brothers. Each of the 5 brothers ran a different part of the company and even though this was a company account and a check was issued for payment, they made all go to each of the brothers and they each explained their function/approval with regards to the entire operation. They liked Al and they liked teaching him the business the old fashion way. Most of the other customers were very predictable on collection day. Some asked you to come back, some gave you bad checks, some paid in pennies and the old ladies always friendly and paid on time. They usually gave a tip and advice on exactly how they wanted the paper delivered. One of the middle age ladies always came to the door dressed in a see through night gown no matter what time of day it was and some people asked if they could pay next month. The price of the paper was 2 dollars and twenty cents per month and yet they all rarely changed their stories. The judgment of the nature of people became apparent to Al and would always serve him well.

Al was always the first one in the school parking lot and his best job benefit was he had time to read the paper. Social integration was front page almost every day no one seemed to have a fix for the problem. Often he would laugh as politicians or political figures of the day would make profound statements on why America was racially divided and what to do to fix it. Al was really afraid that if the great words in the Bible and the US constitution could be ignored because people had a different skin color, what other things about Liberty and Freedom could be ignored. Al also thought of his grandmother's sister. Her family was black. She had married a Black man. Al's grandmother on his father's side was an American Indian and his Grandfather was a totally White Scotchman. Their families loved and respected each other even though one was White and one was Black. This made it impossible for him to imagine hating someone because of their skin color. His family attended their funerals, celebrations and successes. They returned the favors. It was with great interest as he read the words from the mouths of the leaders and problem solvers. When he read of the Congressional debate and filibuster of the Civil rights act he imagined that someday it would all be made into a Broadway Play much like Oklahoma. The senators from the great states of this or that favored ending or continuing segregation of Black and White all had some strange stories. The western and plains states had few blacks in their population and they trashed talked the southern senators and congressmen only to be told of their treatment of Indians, Mexicans, Orientals and non Mormons. The Midwestern people seemed to hate Pollock's which surely meant anyone first generation from mainland Europe and the East Coast States seemed to say Irish with the same tone reserved for white trash drunks. Al failed to see how leadership could emerge from any one part of the United States but he was wrong. The leadership for change came from Texas the last place he expected it. Texas had Black schools, White schools, and Spanish speaking schools and probably thought it a good thing they had sent all the Indians packing to Oklahoma. The next year he would see first hand the Civil Rights movement at its best and worse and he would see how History would totally ignore the real heroes and heap praises awards and money on some of the non participants. People that hid under the bridge of freedom while others walked through hell just to gain an ounce of the human dignity promised to all people in the Bible and the constitution.

The newspaper seemed to have a constant string of stinger stories about a man named James Meredith. It seemed that he single handed led the protest to register voters and integrate the educational institutes of the South. He had been an officer in the Air Force and certainly was not afraid of confrontation. He had been shot with bullets, assaulted, arrested and still he carried on. Many of his marches were alone. Al knew the safety in numbers but this man acted alone in the same tone as the lady Rosa Parks in Montgomery Alabama had in refusing to go to the back of the bus because her skin was black. She didn't refuse to sit in the back of the bus; she refused to stand in the back of the bus while there were empty seats in the front of the bus. Who could not understand this? Al felt closeness to this lady and this man. It was acts committed in the spirit of human nature and if defiance of the law was committed, the laws needed to be changed, yet everyday some congressman or senator put together some string of words as to why the law could not be changed. Another man in the northern states addressed the need for changes to the laws in the name of GOD. This man was hated because he called GOD by the Arabic name of Allah. The newspapers put Malcolm X in the same category reserved for criminals. Still there was another man from Georgia who preached the power of prayer and spoke of his dream when all the children of GOD would one day live in harmony. The newspapers had numerous stingers about this man being a communist and gay. Certainly no one would call James Meredith gay or Godly. They seem to be waiting for the day when a shot or an assault would end his life. Al followed the events of these people's lives as reported by the newspapers. The words of President Johnson were measured but in a non compromising way that said that the wrong must be corrected so America could build a great society and he started to fix the problem by enforcing the law as defined by the US constitution. President Johnson had a shady political background but he knew how to make changes and enforce laws. He understood human dignity and this was probably the reason he had few friends. Al watched and read but he could never imagine the deep hatred that some had for others of a different skin color. He couldn't imagine the hate that existed in most of the states. He often wondered why James Meredith never aligned himself with the other people. He seemed to be a loner and one who lived by President Kennedy's words of "Ask not what your country could do for you, ask what you can do for your country." Al concluded that our country's history had told the problem. The majority of Europeans who came to America in the 1800s had been slaves in their own countries of origin. Most were products of a Feudal system where Serfs were consider a part of the land. Most of the Africans were free people in their country of origin. They were sold into slavery and deported. How could teach freedom and self governance to those who had never known it and how could you deny freedom to those who had always known it.

When Al graduated from high school one of his first jobs away from home was in the Mississippi Delta. The Delta's was home of the KKK and source of the escalated civil rights protest. Memphis is the capital of the Deep South and it seemed the one place where blacks could find non share cropper work and live with some dignity. It was also home of a special brand of music. The kind of music that everyone listened to and could hear the sounds of oppression in both white and black music, the kind of music that gave some comfort to the souls of all people. They made and the radio stations played the kind of music that caused people to think about their struggles in life. Late night radio played music that white people called black music and black people called white people music but music without words allowed everyone to add their own words and dreams and few listeners cared what skin color played the music.

A pipeline job usually doesn't allow employees to live in the same place for several months. Usually pipe liners live in cheap hotels or motels and except for the occasional place that offers bed and breakfast their lives are spent living in cheap motels that usually go empty most of the year. The owners love it because they can charge anything they want to and the pipe liners have no choice except to drive many miles to another cheap motel. The Delta was no different and Al soon learned that ads in the local newspaper for short term rent and bed and breakfast were too difficult. He could not distinguish the color of a person's skin over the telephone and all the towns in the Delta were segregated by Black and White. He also learned that his Texas licenses plates did not help because President Johnson the man causing all the problems was from Texas. He observed noticed that the Delta had a lot of Italian people and a large number of Chinese. The Chinese ran small stores mostly in the Black parts of town and the Italians seemed to own a lot of the businesses. The Chinese seemed to be lost in time and most of the older men still wore their hair in pig tails and spoke only broken English.

Al and his helper didn't mind paying extra for the good motels but finding a good place to eat was a different story. After a few weeks in the middle of the Delta they discovered a small cross roads town with a good restaurant. They become regular customers and befriended the Italian owner and all of her waitresses. The restaurant also served as a bus station, laundry mat, and convenience store. The most unusual part of the Hodge podge of buildings was the fact that it had four restrooms, two dining rooms, two waiting lobbies for the bus station and two laundry mats. Only one kitchen served the restaurant but everything else was clearly marked for Black and White use only. One night as they were having diner the owner made a comment that all the protest and marches were having an effect on her business. Al's helper was a kid from Dallas who had a scholarship to play tennis for the Unv. of Arkansas. He had grown up in Dallas and was working a summer job to earn some bucks for college and to pay for the small Porsche car that he seemed to really enjoy driving down the back roads of Mississippi to follow the ever advancing pipeline. When the owner of the restaurant said that she didn't have anything against black people being equal except it would ruin her business, the helper said that he thought it would be good for business. The owner asked why and he replied that she could save a lot of money on waiting rooms and bathrooms. This comment spoken from the heart caused Al and his helper to be banned from the restaurant permanently. When Al relayed the story to the boss in Dallas he increased their living allowance and they became the joke of other employees because they were banned from anywhere. This was a feat not common to the free spending pipe liners. The long hot summer in the Delta was an experience that two young Texans would never forget. They spent their non working days driving down the highways of Mississippi to witness the freedom marches. The so called freedom marchers didn't seem to have much focus. They mostly looked like a ragged sort of dope smoking hippies and they also looked like paid employees supporting someone else's agenda, not their own. In the faces of a few he could see the pain of being wronged simply because of skin color. Those few stood out in the crowds.

It would not surprising that the biggest and most destructive riots during the civil rights years all occurred in America's Northern cities where economic segregation had cause more loss of dignity and freedom than all the segregated bus stations and water fountains in Mississippi. Nor would it surprise him when he drove through the Delta years later and found a Black population who still had family values, were well educated and spoke proper English with many of them becoming business owners. Nor did it surprise him to go back to the crossroads town and go into the old restaurant only to discover that it was nor just a run down gas station and a cheap one with one filthy bathroom. Not even the new owner being a Pakistani surprised him. When he thought of the blood, sweat, tears and prayers spent on civil rights in America he wondered where such a noble and just cause went wrong.

Meredith just faded away and few people even remember him, the Muslim preacher was gunned down by his own people, the Baptist preacher was also gunned down in Memphis a few years later. No one is sure who gunned him down but a lot of fingers point to a branch of the government. His underlings went on to derail the real issue of civil rights; all became rich and infamous mostly serving their own causes and thirty years later their greatest crusades would be to abolish the N word from the English language. Mostly he wondered why so much effort had not helped his cousins who were still socially and economically discriminated against. He was convinced that to right the civil rights ship in America there needed to be other leaders like President Kennedy and Johnson who could see clearly and that seemed very unlikely. Right and wrong would become a position of being politically correct rather than interpretation of the Bible and the U.S. constitution. It seemed that Americas only hope as defined by the politicians were to make more unenforceable laws and to build more jails. This seemed to be a way for gutless politicians to separate themselves from people and it seemed the politicians were afraid of people.

CHAPTER 6

1964 THE BIG HOUSE

The war in Viet Nam was heating up in 1964. America was still drafting men into the Armed forces and they were drafting them in record numbers. It was the first time that Americans had used TV to report news of a war. The public was hesitant to buy into a war so far away with such a foreign country. The memory of war in Korea was still fresh and was still being referred to as a United Nations police action. Every one who served in Korea knew it was no police action. Al's first cousin had been awarded a Silver Star for shooting down two Migs; you don't associate Russian Migs and Silver Stars with police actions. Americans knew little about South East Asia and most of them didn't want to know.

AL had been working for Brown & Root in the new owner Halliburton's machine shop in Duncan Oklahoma. It was a long way from home and the Okies at Halliburton didn't seem so strange but Duncan was not a prosperous town, most of the people living there were dirt poor but most employees had lots of accumulated only Halliburton stock. Halliburton was a private company and stock was given to employees and bought back upon their retirement or planned departure from the company. After the company went public these employees would be millionaires despite being dirt poor most of their lives. Labor turn over at Halliburton was non-existent. Drinking alcohol was allowed in Duncan but only in private clubs.

Al's non work time was spent in the rented room of a boarding house reading history books or talking to other employees. The most popular guest was the brother of comedian George Goble. He looked exactly like his brother. When Mr. Goble wasn't telling stories about his brother George he was on a drinking binge. Another famous guest was a big Indian named Manes who was a descendant of the father of Texas, Sam Houston. He was descended from Sam's Indian family. He constantly complained about the low pay at Halliburton. Skilled craftsmen made $3.75 per hour and minimum wage was $1.25 per hour but oilfield pay was considerably higher when the rigs were working. Al's boss was a Czech Bohemian from the Gulf Coast of Texas. He was a retired journey machine man from Dow Chemical near Clute Texas where he helped build and run the Chlorine and magnesium facilities built for World War II. He was all business and only talked about work except to tell Al he was retired from Dow but was still working to help his recently divorced daughter get back on her feet. He checked everything Al did until he had confidence in him, then he just depended on him to do it right.

The boarding house they lived in was an old mansion with a dozen bedrooms and a couple of recently added toilets. It was near work and also near downtown Lawton. There were only a couple of motels outside of town and their rates were too high. Meals were served punctual and the entire boarding house was full of other Brown & Root employees. The lady running the boarding house had no sense of humor and she invented zero tolerance. Even Mr. Gobbles drinking binges were not at the boarding house. It was his recovery place. Mr. Manes didn't like the food and let everyone know about it. Not too much Manes liked except Al. He liked Al because Al was part Indian and he grew up in East Texas near where Sam Houston spent his final years. Manes had lived all his life in Oklahoma and he had felt the sting of racial prejudices all his life. He was living in a boarding house with a bunch of white men who talked too much and drank too much and that made him uncomfortable. Non of the Brown and Root boys wanted to get cross ways with Manes, he was much too big and strong and he always kept a persona that seem to say "I am ready". Al had never felt the sting of racial prejudices even though his grandmother was full blooded Indian because his father had raised him and his brothers on a piece of land that bordered a wild life management area and a National forest, not so far from the only Indian reservation in Texas. White folks lived a long way from where he grew up. Al and his brothers loved to fight but his father did not tolerate fighting so their after school bouts with school bullies were always kept quiet. His father had a simple rule, if you get into a fight for any reason "I will whip you." His mother had another rule, "if you lose a fight I will whip you" The very thought of losing a fight and getting 3 whippings made fighting very difficult to justify but him and his brothers loved a good fight. Al was only 19 years old and most of the Brown & Root boys were seasoned construction workers in their 30's and 40's but Al also had an air that seems to say "I am ready" so he caught little flack from the boys. Most of the construction workers had done time in jail and some in prison. They didn't seem ashamed and seemed to wear their records like an old gunfighter wore his guns with notched handles. Most of the history books Al read at the boarding house were about the Oklahoma Indians, it seemed very few Indians were native to Oklahoma. His curiosity about Oklahoma Indians was perked when a hometown friend of his had married an Indian girl. He was completely shut out by all the white boys and was eventually fired. He never spoke to Manes about racial hatred but Manes knew he was part Indian and Manes knew Al was always ready to fight, so he took him under his wing and helped him with the hard jobs. Al seemed to get all the hard jobs. Most Brown & Root boys loved to steal tools, Al and Manes didn't steal and both carefully marked and checked their own tools. Good tools meant doing a good job. It seemed that construction was the one of the few places that ex cons could find work. Duncan didn't have many construction types so most of the construction workers were imported from out of town and most were from the Houston area and a large percent of the construction workers were ex cons.

When the project neared completion Manes ask Al to go with him to the next town from Duncan named Lawton. It was also home of a large Army base. He showed Al the jail that had housed the Great Chief Geronimo and his Grave. Neither made comment but Al was surprised to see his first Army base. Soldiers of all shapes and sizes filled the town on the chilly Saturday afternoon. Most of the soldiers had shaved heads and seemed to be looking only in one direction. It seemed that the short drive back to Duncan that a dark cloud was following the old Ford. Winter was coming and the air was becoming cold. The next week their boss told them they would be finishing with work in Duncan, so get ready to go home. Manes had already found a job on a drilling rig. The boss told Al to call the Houston office within two weeks. Al defined the two weeks as when he got home and was ready to go back to work. The following week they all left with out much a do. A simple hand shake and some kind words of appreciation was the end of their working together and a good bye. Al made the drive back to Texas and it was slow. The sight of pine trees and rolling sand hills were a welcomed sight. He had saved a pocket full of money, knew there was a job waiting and really wanted to spend time with his high school girlfriend, she would be a junior and they had a lot of talking to do. They had talked about getting married as all their friends were doing but both seemed uncertain of themselves. It seemed that after marriage all Al's friends became slaves of the only places in their hometown to find steady work. The paper mill and the foundry were the only big companies in town. All small business were family owned and never hired a non family member. Al's father had worked at the foundry for 35 years. His girl friends father had worked at the paper mill for 31 years. They wanted a different way but no path was apparent and they didn't have to decide what to do until she graduated. The pocket full of money would last 6 months if he was lucky, he wasn't because as he drove into his fathers drive way the engine of his car made a loud noise that was metal to metal. His father told him the engine was burned up and the rods were knocking, it needed to be rebuilt. Maybe he could just find another engine at a junk yard. Weeks passed and finally his grandfather came to see them and told him of a mechanic who could rebuild the engine like new. They towed the car to his grandparents house, but three months later the car was the same because Al and his grandfather caught fishing fever. Fishing fever was cured when Al's father gave him a long talk about living off other people and paying his own way. Al thought this meant working at the foundry. He finally made the call to Houston that his boss had told him to do but he was questioned why he took so long to call and they informed him to call back in four more months. The car went to the mechanic and he advised that it would take six weeks to overhaul the engine. Grandpa told him that he had found him a job. A renter in Grandpa's rent house worked for the Texas Prison system. He was a truck driver but was told that the state was going to be hiring a lot of people to work for the prison system. He gave Al an application and helped him fill it out. Lack of law enforcement experience seemed a sure out because Al reasoned that no one under 25 years old would be hired by the state of Texas. He was wrong. Seemed he was the first person hired out of the 500 applicants. Al thought his interview with the State psychologist would surely flame him out. Al had told him point blank that his relationship with his mother and father were none of his business and he refused to answer his senseless questions. Al also was sure that his answer to "could he kill a man" wasn't what the shrink wanted to hear. Al said he didn't know if he could and did not want to reason about such things as murder even in self defense. Al was shaken when he entered the prison and the large steel doors were closed. He didn't see any convicts that scared him but being locked up sure did. Why did all the prison hiring people lock themselves up inside the prison?

The new director of the Texas prisons system was about to implement reform to the Texas penal system and he wanted young people with no experience so he could train them his way. The new director had been a Methodist Minister and his slogan was "incarceration is for the confinement of the punished, not the punishment of the confined". All convicts would have a job, take a bath each day, eat three meals a day with a knife and fork and they would all change to clean clothes every day. Texas convicts wore starched white uniforms. Al was the first person hired and was told to go home get one set of clothes, personal toilet items and return early the next morning. He was being sent to the Prison training academy. He was also told that his pay would be 360 dollars per month and he would be in training camp for 6 weeks. As his grandpa drove them home Al calculated that that was about 500 bucks which was more than enough to get the engine rebuilt and almost half of the four months before he could call Brown and root for a job. Seemed things were looking up. He was so wrong again …… …

The training academy had been fun and interesting. Texas Prison system was actually 13 different large prison farms. They produced enough food and cash crops to more than pay for the expense of housing some twenty five thousand convicts. They raised their own cows, pigs, chickens and vegetables to feed all the convicts, guards and most of the nearby county police officials. They had housed some famous convicts, had a storied history and were one of the last prison systems in America to use old sparkie, the famous electric chair, to execute condemned convicts. Most of the prison farms were in the Trinity River bottom or the Brazos river bottom. Some of the best farming land in the state. It seemed that the State of Texas had acquired most of the land for the prisons after the American Civil war when the plantation owners could not pay taxes. Tons of cotton was produced as a cash crop. Acres of maize and corn was produced for cash crops and feed for livestock. The Prison system was not only self sufficient but produced income money for the state of Texas.

Classes in fire arms and self defense mixed with police identification techniques and some legal training filled the training days. One class on convict language was held and provided some insight on the new job. When a convict said "on the job" it meant he had to use the toilet. The trainees were moved inside the prison for the final two weeks of training. Al was amazed to see the living arrangements inside a prison. The prison being used for training was the newest one in the system. Neat cell blocks that were well lighted and each hall way had a series of painted lines. When convicts were inside the building they could walk only on one of the painted lines and were observed by guards at all times. The prisons were all segregated but they were separated by age, race and offence. The training prison had first time offenders, white and Mexican and under the age of 25. During Al's first reading of criminal records he spotted a white boy, age 24 who had worked for Brown & Root. He had stolen too much equipment and was doing 5 years. When Al visited his cell he saw a tough looking young man who had just completed thirty days of solitary confinement. His eyes were still adjusting from the 30 days of total darkness and in spite of the pictures hung in his cell of his wife and small son, he seemed to be totally defeated. Seemed he had been sent to solitary confinement for walking outside the painted lines. Al looked closely at him and determined that he had not worked with him at Duncan.

Al had done well with the self defense classes and was assigned to work in the kitchen. Kitchens were dangerous places to work because of all the knives. He was amazed that they could cook 3 meals a day for seven hundred convicts, serve the meals and do it all seven days a week, year round. The pure logistics of food seemed impossible because the old lady at the boarding house in Duncan seemed to have a lot of trouble feeding twenty people. Never enough food and always over or under cooked but here the giant steam pots and ovens made it seem easy. Convicts entered the cafeteria in an orderly fashion, ate in a timely manner and departed to work or back to their cells in a straight evenly spaced group that always followed the painted lines. Part of Al's duties was to count silverware after the cons had finished eating; each convict must show the knives, forks and spoons before turning in for washing. The Sgt had told him that this would be the main source of making hand made knives or shanks and must be monitored. In the past convicts had to eat with their hands to avoid such risk but the new director had ordered that each convict must use a knife, fork and spoon and must sit up straight and use the silverware properly when eating. Prior to this the convicts were forced to eat with their hands because they would steal the knives, forks and spoons to hone into shanks for weapons.

One day in Al's inspection of the food pantries Al say something that shocked him to his core. He entered the pantry and in the back he saw one convict on his knees performing oral sex on another convict. Al froze and the two convicts quickly turned and walked past him. One of them said to Al "I am going to be here 35 years". When he returned from the pantry the Capt of the mess sing operations asked him if he had learned anything interesting. Al said yes and told the Captain what he had seen. The Captain wanted him to describe the two convicts and in spite of the identification training Al could not identify them. After telling the Captain everything he had seen the Captain pilled out a slap jack from his desk. The slap jack was a spoon shaped piece of leather that fit around the hand and it had a one inch diameter steel ball bearing inside, Al had seen one before because his father had one that he used when he was running a dance hall. His father had used it to encourage drunks in his bar to follow his directions. A short time later the captain had returned with the two convicts which Al immediately recognized, one had been Italian and the other had been a blond haired white boy. Al was embarrassed because immediately all the other trainees had started the joke that Al was going to be the top in the class and receive the promised Sergeant stripe for being the top trainee because he had caught two queers. The mess captain had told Al that all homosexuals were housed in the same cell blocks and worked only with other homosexuals because they would be treated horribly by the other convicts and the convicts would stop eating in protest of homosexuals working in the kitchen. Al was totally embarrassed by the incident and when he was congratulated in the training class he couldn't look anyone in the eye. His only thought was I really need to find a telephone and call Brown & Root. Prior to this Al's only experience with homosexuals was watching his Uncles new prize bull gives himself a blow job. The bull would wrap himself around the scratching post, bend his head towards his rear and perform oral sex on him self. When Al's uncle didn't receive his usual low number of newborn calves he remembers his father seeing the bull do his oral thing and joking with his brother that he thought he knew why no all of the cows had calves. Al's uncle was so mad he sold he bull for slaughter. He could have gotten more money by just selling him for a good looking bull but he sold him for hamburger. Al had hoped that these two convicts would fare much better by just being moved to the gay dorm and working in the flower beds around the prison.

During the last week of training each trainee was asked to give the three prisons that they wanted to be assigned to work at. Al wrote "no preference". He had no intention of working at any prison. The five hundred dollars were almost in his pocket and the car was waiting at the mechanics garage, fixed ready to run. The call to Brown & Root was not encouraging. He was told that they were terminating people in the states but they had received a government contract to build things in Viet Nam. Al was not old enough to be sent to Viet Nam to work. Seems you had to be 25 years old but it seemed Al was old enough to still be on active file with his local Draft board.

The prison personnel in charge of making job assignments must have thought his worries were over when he read Al's choice of assignments which said "No preference". Seems he knew just such a prison for Al to work at.

Clement Unit was located near the Texas gulf coast and was one of the smaller prison farms. A place Al had never heard mentioned although it was near the first Anglo settlement in Texas. Seems the Spanish government had a sense of humor because when pressured to allow Anglo settlements in Texas they made the Anglos convert to the Catholic religion and then gave them land in the alligator filled swamps of the Gulf Coast. The Karanawki Indians who were living there when the Spanish first arrived had put fear of God into the Spanish because they were cannibals. Seems the alligators and mosquitoes were also a problem but just incase the gators, bugs and disease didn't kill you they also had major hurricanes that wiped out everything standing. Not a good place to live but it was all the Spanish offered the Anglos. It was located just up the Brazos River from the port city of Velasco. The prison housed 750 convicts who were first offenders, black, age 19 to 25. A good portion of the convict population would come from the larger Texas cities. It was an old prison and had no cells, no painted lines. Inside the prison was exactly like an Army barracks with stacks of double deck bunk, each bed had a wooden locker at the foot of the beds. It was divided up into a total of nine tanks or dorms. No solid walls inside the building but the tanks were separated by a wall of bars. Each of the non trustee tanks had up to 80 convicts and a trustee whose job was to keep the tank clean and orderly. Inside the building during the non outside working hours there was a total of one security guard. During the day the Warden and assistant warden had offices that were supported by a female secretary. The inside guard controlled all door openings and closing. This was limited to when someone got sick or had an outside night job. Only the laundry and the mess hall operated full speed at night. The laundry had no security guard and the mess hall had one officer who also served as the chief cook and night Sergeant. Outside the building were large chain link fences with barbed wire on top and three security towers positioned to see the entire fence area. These towers had armed guards. The inside guard and the night Sgt were not armed but there was tear gas available if a riot broke out and only the security guard had a gas mask. Al was assigned to the inside security position. He worked the evening shift which started at four pm and finished at midnight. Normally the convicts would work outside until 5 or 6 pm then return to the building where they would shower, change clothes, and go straight to the mess hall. From the mess hall they would go to their assigned tanks. Al opened the doors for them to return to their tanks. Each Tank had a TV and they could watch it until 10 pm and then shortly there after Al would turn off the lights after they were all in their bunks and each trustee had made a final count of convicts. Normally the convicts were so tired they went to sleep before the lights were turned out. By 11 pm not a sound could be heard except 750 people sleeping. Incredibly when it got dark and quiet Al would read a book but the Warden insisted that Al read the records of the convicts including court records. Al made it a habit of reading the files he got directly from the wardens desk because Al knew the Warden also read the same files. The last call to Brown & Root had not been good. Seems they were only hiring people to work in Viet Nam. The summer of 64 would be a long hot one because the prison did not have air conditioning.

The prison had a barber shop for officers. The barber shop had 2 full time barbers and a shoe shine boy. The two barbers were both convicted for armed robbery and serving thirty years. Al read their files and noticed that one of them was from Chicago. Most officers had their hair cut once a week and the style was a very close cut military. Al usually got his hair cut on Wednesday and the barber shop was usually empty. After reading the barber named Jim from Chicago he noticed that he was tried and convicted in a very small county in the extreme North Texas, just across the Oklahoma state line. The records always told what they were tried for and convicted of but it never seem to say why they did it. The barber told Al that he had followed a diamond salesman all the way from Chicago and finally decided to rob him in his motel room. Unfortunately the motel room was in Texas. Al asked him if the seven plus years in Texas prisons would stop him from stealing. The barber said no because he had been a thief all his life and when he wasn't in prison he was stealing. All his friends were thieves and that had been his way of life. Then he said "I will never again steal in Texas because the time is just too hard." The shoe shine boy looked up and laughed. The shoe shine boy was a small black man. He had trembling nervous voice that seem to crack when he spoke. His eyes were deep set and he never seemed to look in one direction too long. He appeared to be in his late twenties and not the type of convict that would attract attention. During his work in the barber shop he always seemed to stay busy. Most of the officers brought all their shoes and boots for him to shine. They would drop off items in the morning and pick them up the next day. The only clue that Kenny the shoe shine boy was an unusual convict was the way the barbers looked at him. They rarely spoke to Kenny and seemed to show him the kind of respect that a cowboy shows a rattle snake. The barbers were both free speakers while they were working in the barber shop but Al noticed that they never spoke to or about Kenney. Some of the officers came in for a morning or afternoon shave. Al thought about the danger of having a man locked up in prison wielding a straight razor around his neck. One bad thought or slip or freak out of any kind and the officer's throat would be cut. Seemed to risky for Al to consider but still he wondered why some guards allowed the convicts to shave them.

After several months of reading files Al found Kenny's file. It read like a mystery book. His sentence was 99 years with a no parole clause. Even the no parole clause was different. It specified that Kenney's prison assignments and all case appeals or pleas for parole must be sent to the Judge who sentenced him. Kenney was from Dallas but his court of record was from a small town just south of Dallas. The court records and trial files were full of specific instructions, it seemed that Kenny had confessed and the trial was merely a sentencing and Kenny had barely missed the death sentence. He was truly condemned for life. Never again would he breathe free air. Al thought that death would have been more humane.

All the other files Al read were pale compared to Kenny's. Al read it several times during the next few months and still there was not a clue as to why Kenney had killed the teen age girl and then dumped her body in the small town. Kenny had a good school record, came from a good home, had no previous arrest and he was religious. Al had caught a glimpse of his Bible that he always kept inside his shoe shine box. Al learned to visit Kenny while the barbers were out of the barber shop and to talk to him about his sentence. Kenny really did not know why he killed the girl; he reasoned that after them running away for a weekend, the drugs and alcohol formed a deadly combination. They had gone several days without sleep and then had some argument. Kenny said it seemed like a dream when he was choking her and when he realized she was dead he became very afraid, so afraid that he drove out of town and dumped her body. When he returned home his parents and her parents questioned him and he said he didn't know. A few days later when her body was discovered, Kenny confessed everything that he remembered. Case closed, Kenny was to be locked up forever and ever. He had no visitors on his list and no one on his mail list. Kenny was as dead as a man can get but yet he wasn't dead at all. After Al had talked for many days to Kenny did he began to thaw and he told Al of what his life was like before the murder. Kenny had been a good child and his parents had been proud of him. Seemed his girlfriend and her family had been friends of his family. She was dead and so was Kenny. Nothing could change it. Every time Al called Brown & Root he got the idea that all arrows pointed to Viet Nam.

Al quietly enrolled in college. His studies included every class that ended in "ogy" or had ogy imbedded in its title. During the next 2 years Al had accumulated enough college credits from the Community college, the Jr. College and finally the University to graduate with a couple of "ogy" degrees. He received only A's and sometimes he had to beg to take advanced courses. Al had known that the men he worked with at Brown and Rood were worse people than most of the convicts. What was the real reason some were free men and some were convicts? Al didn't have a clue but he did remember what the prison shrink had told him. He said that all convicts had only one thing in common and that was the inability to establish a patterned way of life. What to hell did that mean,

Al had never followed a pattern in his life, and at least there was no pattern he recognized. Still he was sure there was a real answer and he wanted to find it. His graduate courses seemed to confirm his suspicions that any professional "ogy" major was expected to motivate and condition people, not to fix the broken ones. People whose jobs were to fix the broken ones were on the lower pay and less motivated list and it seemed to Al that they were really trying to just understand themselves.

The letter from Al's draft board was a welcome relief. It left no room for doubt in saying "report to" and be "prepared for". The bus ride to the Army processing center was a one way trip. Al was finally going to Viet Nam but not with Brown & Root. He was still too young for them to hire him for work in Viet Nam. As the bus carrying the recruits into the Army Fort for basic training Al sat on the bus silently wishing that his friends Kenny and Manes were going there with him.

Chapter 7

1998 Siberia

A l had retired from the oil company and the benefits were called a golden parachute. Free insurance, lots of cash, company stock and no reason to join the newly merged company. He was 58 years old and tired of corporate bull shit. He bought a cattle ranch, cows and all the toys. His brother had complained for years about how much money he had lost in the cattle business. Al's main goal was to turn a profit. He experimented with different breeds of cows and finally settled on Brangus because they fit the land best. The breed was developed as three eights Brahma and five eights Angus in the river deltas of Louisiana and they could handle heat, humid weather and mosquitoes. Al's brother had gotten in to embryo transplants and artificial breeding. Al thought that nature was best. For two years Al's neighbors watched as he experimented, then in the second year they all noticed that Al's calves sold for 25 percent more at the local market. They also noticed that he had healthy strong cows. At this point Al had created a second source of revenue and filing taxes were more difficult. He was bored and retirement was not so enjoyable. Most of the work improving the ranch had been done. His friend Raffel an illegal Mexican had taught him how to doctor the cows. Raffel had been hired by his neighbor but Al's neighbor did not treat Raffel as an equal. He considered him as an illegal Mexican. Raffel had become Al's friend who was always there to help when a cow got stuck in the mud having a baby calve. Raffel lived in an old travel trailer and had no transportation into town. Al rounded up a heater and a TV for Raffel. Raffel drank a lot when he wasn't working. He managed to keep a working cell phone and his children in Mexico called him a few times a week. Al thought Raffel drank because of the struggles his family was having in Mexico and he was almost helpless to assist them in dealing with their sufferings. Al had given up drinking after his last work stint in Russia. He had known and worked with too many alcoholics. He had seen lives destroyed and he had even seen the effects it has on children whose mothers drank during their pregnancies. The Russians had drinking problems that reminded Al of the American Indian drinking problem he had seen in Oklahoma. Still in spite of his intolerance for alcohol and drunks Al came to like Raffel. He often carried him to buy his beer and on special occasions he gave him tequila. Raffel trusted Al and hid nothing from Al. When his boss didn't pay him, he stole his ranchers' cows, sold its hay and feed and he also ran a safe house for his Mexican friends who had made it safely across the border. Raffel was good people and an unfortunate victim of years of Mexican corruption and not caring for its own people. He was proud and seemingly did not begrudge his own mistreatment. Most of all Al admired his love for his native country and his family. Raffel was a very good cowboy and a friend to Al whether he was drunk or sober.

Al was bored and knew he could trust Raffel with his cows and the ranch, so Al welcomed the phone call from his old boss requesting Al join him in Siberia. The boss had told him that the company had screwed up again. They had traded for some oil properties and hadn't done their homework. Production was half of what was promised. Cost of doing business was too high but the upside was the Russian owner had not known the geology and could not sustain any development. Russian drilling rigs were very cheap compared to US rates and he wanted to do some major exploration and come up with the real oil fields that the Russians had been drilling around for years. Al asked if he had been in charge of the acquisition team and he said yes but the company had assigned some Dick Weeds to him and they had not been honest with him. Al asked him if he would be in Siberia and he said "no" that he would be in Moscow. Al asked if there would be any Americans with him and he said "only one." Do you remember Paul? Al remembered Paul very well and was friends with him if anyone could be friends with Paul. Paul had been raised by the Salvation Army in Indiana. He made his way through Indiana State by playing basketball and selling Pizza. His best and most reliable customers had been a couple of whore houses that had some strong connections to the town mayor. Paul knew the oil business and was very good at sniffing out oil but he was really good with getting it to market. Paul had been married to the sister of the CEO to a large oil company. He had been through a dirty divorce and left Houston for Russia after having a torrid affair with his manager's secretary. Paul was the kind of employee who was too good to lose to the competition but too bad for corporate image. Al had met him five years earlier in the Russian Far East. Paul had several affairs and finally married one of the local girls. He spoke only Russian and lived off the land. He had convinced his much younger bride to study geology. Al liked Paul but was never sure why. Sometimes in their staff meetings Al would imagine Paul standing on a street corner ringing the Salvation Army bell. He often felt like he did when he dropped money into the bell ringer's pot. No matter how much or little you dropped into the pot their expression seemed to say, "You could have given more". Seems it had been Paul who was requesting the Boss to get Al on the job.

Al knew the boss had been much too easy with the pay. He gave Al more than Al intended to ask for or expected to be paid. The one thing Al did demand and get was a full time personal Russian translator. Al hoped it would be a good looking woman, someone that he could spoil and have a romantic affair with, but the boss was one up. Al's translator was a North Korean male who had grown up in St Petersburg and was perfectly content to do nothing all day.

Al joined his translator and flew on to Siberia after a one night stay in Moscow and being unable to see the boss. Paul would join them at the old government hotel in the morning. At least the hotel was warm. The hotel fire alarm went off at three a.m., just after the bar had closed. All guests were evacuated and stood in the freezing cold while hotel employees and Emergency Management people checked for fire and determined that it was a false alarm. The translator came in handy interpreting hotel guest comments. Al's favorite was made by a young Russian who was still drunk and was standing next to a very good looking girlfriend. He told the EMP that "if you made us stand in the cold any longer, I guaranteed that there would be a real fire later tonight."

When Paul arrived at the hotel to pick Al and the translator up it was at 6 am on the minute. He was all smiles but offered only friendly conversation in presence of the translator. Al took notice. He had heard of the reports translators made daily but had never experienced it. In the Russian Far East no one seemed to care enough to report anything. The Russian Far East had been a good experience and communist was not a good word. They had been occupied by Japan and much too close to Manchuria during WWII. Sakhalin Island had been originally settled as a penal colony under the last Czar. The Russian homeland for Jews that Stalin had created was also located in the Russian Far East, seven or eight time zones ahead of Moscow. The world paid little attention to Sakhalin Island until oil was discovered and FLIGHT KAL007 was shot down. Siberia would be a different story. This was the wild/wild West and only the strong ruled and survived. Fortunes were made and lost on a weekly basis.

The boss had told Al that all oil companies had difficulties getting Russian employees to relocate to Siberia. He was allowing employees to work two weeks in Siberia and two weeks off with pay. Something he had learned while he worked offshore Louisiana. The translator was a hard core commie. The first week at work was usual oil patch stuff, production people needing more chemicals, drillers getting drill bits stuck in the hole, logistics bitching about the weather, and accountants trying to follow the money. It seemed there were too many Russian geologists studying maps and worrying about drilling locations. Paul had insisted Al share his office and the translator would reside in a downstairs office until Al needed him. They both knew that Paul's office was bugged but at least now they knew who would be listening and who they would be reporting to.

Drilling season in Siberia occurs only when the temperature reaches minus 25 deg C. The remainder of the year most of the country side is swamp and impassible by roads. The town they were living in was located about 1500 miles up the Ob River and the place where the Iratush River joined the Ob. The Ob is longer and bigger than the Mississippi and the Iratush is about the same size and length as the Missouri. In Russia most rivers run from South to North, the Ob ran almost straight north to the Arctic Ocean. The Russians had settled exiled people in Siberia by bring settlers by boat up the rivers during the summers and picking out land that was high and dry. They would come back the following year to see how many if any survived. It had created a hearty and healthy breed of people. During the past 300 years every time Mother Russia had been in war, the people of Siberia had risen to defend Russia. Al felt these were the real Russian people and was not too surprised by their friendliness and overall healthy looks. The absence of policemen was also not too surprising.

Had the town been settled in a location that permitted over land travel it would have been much like St Louis? Unfortunately the town never grew into anything other than a regional center for Communist control and most of the original population was reindeer herders with a curious mix of "deported to Siberia" Cossacks. It was a clean efficient town and obviously a proud one. These people were survivors. Labor shortages had allowed importation of labor from other parts of Russia and the world. The population was almost 40,000 people and probably a mix of 5,000 of indigenous people that appeared to be drunken nomadic reindeer herders. Several thousand Turkish contractors had been contracted to make new apartment buildings. The Turks kept to themselves because a small population in the town was Armenians. Al noted that the indigenous people looked very much Korean but with smaller bone features. Al also noted that most of the small businesses in town were owned by Armenians. The kind of people he had only seen in Hollywood. The town had preserved its buildings from early log houses through the Soviet square apartment buildings to the modern glass and steel.

Siberian towns were supplied and survived by river boat traffic and small airports. This town was no different except it had two major rivers that both started a long way to the East in the Mountains of Kazakhstan. Plutonium produced upstream in the secret Soviet centers during the cold war had polluted the rivers but during the spring thaw the rivers grew by miles wide and swept away every thing that wasn't tied down. The rivers delta contained very few high land masses. Al mentioned to Paul that it all looked like South Louisiana frozen over. Paul told Al that when the rivers froze the Russian military would make ice bridges and heavy trucks and equipment could travel freely to all the country side. During the frozen season the company could truck pipe and heavy equipment from the nearest rail center. The nearest railroad was several hundred miles away.

Ice bridges to cross the rivers were made by aligning a string of barrages across the river then pumping water from the non frozen part of river bottom to the tops of the barrages. The ice bridges were frozen lengths of solid ice that was more than twenty feet thick and several miles long. Paul told Al to plan all drilling rig moves during the ice season and to start activities after the average temperature had remained at minus 25 C for one week. Paul also told Al to make sure the drilling islands made of dredged and compacted river sand must be higher than the flood plane elevations of the rivers and constructed properly so they wouldn't wash away during the spring thaw. The drilling pads were small islands and must support not only the drilling rigs but all producing facilities required to get the oil to market. Al proceeded to plan a drilling program for 19 drilling rigs and 104 new wells. After weeks of work he had a plan that would allow 109 wells and use only 14 drilling rigs. Al's plan had produced a savings of seven million dollars to the company's annual budget and gave the geologist five more possibilities to find new oil. Henry the Canadian drilling manager was not happy and voiced his opinion to the boss long before he told Al why he thought the plan to aggressive.

Henry was a surprise to Al because Al expected Paul to be the only Westerner he would work with. Henry was a short squatty Canadian who looked like a hockey goalie. He had come with the company acquisition and had been in Siberia much too long. He was a Canadian from Alberta and had spent most of his life in the oil patch but the last 12 years in Siberia. He was short, ill tempered and crippled from falling down a flight of icy stairs. Henry was a tyrant and in spite of his Polish ancestry he envisioned himself as King of Drilling in Siberia. He knew everything about Russian drilling rigs and he had been there and done that. All of his away time from work time was spent in Africa. He was very much like Paul except Henry wasn't married and constantly hit on the Russian women and never considered a vacation outside Africa. Ludmuller a big boned divorced Cossack was his standby. He openly administered his Russian drilling contractors with threats and promises of bonuses and kickbacks and he didn't trust Al or Paul. He spoke Russian oil patch language but hesitated to do so because Paul seemed to enjoy correcting his Russian grammar. Paul's looks at Henry reminded Al of the Salvation Army bell ringer whose look made one feel guilty for not dropping change from both pockets in to the kettle. Henry had his feelings hurt because he had worked on the drilling plan for more than a year and in six weeks Al had stolen his thunder and forced him to do more work or give back some budgeted money.

Al made a trip to Moscow to show the boss his work. The flight to Moscow had been emotional for Al. It seems that Americans had learned the door to adoption ran through Moscow. Childless couples would pay more than twenty five thousand to adopt a Russian orphan. The children were not only white; they were usually beautiful and well disciplined. It was a business ran by the Russian mafia and few bones were made about it. They could pay local orphanages and corrupt government officials to allow the adoption by foreigners. Every flight from Siberia to Moscow had American couples dragging Russian children back to Moscow and after the final shakedown for additional money the couples carried their new children back to the states. Al had gotten into much trouble because he challenged the corruption of the Catholic Church and their adoption practices as a means to finance their church funding. Al and the translator were seated in the back of the plane. Shortly after take off a 9 or 10 year old boy began screaming and running up and down the isles of the plane. Al looked at the American couple and noticed a few things that told everything. They were dressed in clothing that said expensive winter clothing but not expensive enough to keep warm in Siberia. They were definitely from Colorado or the area and did not look like a happy family. The couple looked like middle age hippies who had finally yearned to have a family because they were bored with each other. They had two children, the 9 year old who was running down the isles of the plane and a 3 or 4 year old who was chewing on a granola bar. Al asked the translator to tell him what the 9 year old was saying. The translator looked coldly at Al and began. "I don't want to go to America". Leave me alone" "Somebody help me, I don't want to go". Al spotted the Russian mafia handler and burned holes through him. How could anyone be such a modern day slave trader? How could all the Russian passengers simply ignore the child? How could they sleep knowing the mafia was selling their children but mostly Al thought about what he would do if it were an American child leaving the states for a life in Russia? The translator saw Al's eyes shedding tears and he stopped translating.

In Moscow Al knew the boss would not be impressed with his new plan and he wasn't. That's why he had hired Al, so he wouldn't be impressed. Al spent most of his time in Moscow with his old friend

Jim who was the company's Chief geologist. We had gained five new wells, now exactly where did we need to drill. Jim told Al that there were two spots that the boss had rejected but he thought that high potential for oil. Jim was a timid person and would not fight with corporate or the boss. He was a very good geologist and had made the company millions of dollars. In Moscow he lived alone and walked almost ten miles to the office. On bad days when ice made it difficult to walk he would take the subway in spite of their recent ticket increase and increased terrorist threats to the subway. He explained to Al that he and Paul had different views on where the main oil was located. Paul had thought the fields were similar to the East Texas fields but he thought they mirrored the Kansas oil fields. Jim said he would give Al the locations for the new five wells. Al promised to make Jim's new wells a top priority. This wasn't the first time Al and Jim had pulled an end run on corporate. Both understood that neither Paul nor the boss could be told of their new 5 well plan. Al was pretty sure Henry would screw up a few wells just to show he could, it wouldn't matter because Al had studied all drilling locations and would make sure Henry's sabotage would have little impact on the overall drilling program, if he screwed up production numbers he would answer to Paul. Al imagined Henry standing on a cold dark street corner, ringing the Salvation Army bell.

In Moscow Al and the boss dined on a pound of US prime beef. The boss told Al that now days his job was about half work and half dealing with Russian government officials. They had made him "the Russian oilman of the year" and some people in Houston were not happy. He told Al that the Russians had also awarded him their Medal of Freedom for the second time and he had yet to tell anyone in Houston because they are still mad at him for receiving the first one. Al knew that the boss was the first American to receive such an honor from the Russians and he knew that the bosses' biggest strengths were he treated all Russians with great respect and dignity. He believed that doing good for Russian people was the same as doing good for the entire world? It didn't hurt anything that his

Russian mistress was related to Boris Yeltzin and she was not only very good looking, she was the best publicists in Moscow. Al asked how she was doing. The boss's eyes smiled and said that she was fine. He didn't even question Al's meetings with Jim, but he asked Al how the Russian translator was working out. Al gave him a look of disgust but he didn't comment. Al had sent his translator home to Saint Petersburg for the weekend.

The overnight flight back to Siberia was uneventful and the translator's conjugal visit had obviously gone well. Al thought about Jim's new wells, two of them would be drilled in a location that had no access to a pipeline and if a discovery was made the oil would have to be trucked across the Ob River. This meant the yield would be only for six months per year and subject to trucks breaking down. The company could not get permits to make a pipeline river crossing. The Russians government thought it to dangerous and the environmentalist were dead set against it. A new discovery would add to proven reserves and if Jim was correct it would be a completely new field that could be sold to the nearest oil company on that side of the river. Yukos would be that oil company because they were located just to the North of the new wells but Yukos was going to hell in a hand basket. Seems a few Russian Jews had come out and bought up most of the small new independent oil companies that had been created when ownership of the companies had been transferred from the Soviet Union to Russian employees. Seems they paid far too little money and had used extortion. Most importantly Yukos had become the largest oil company in Russia and had done most of their banking offshore. Taxes and royalty records were shady. They had hired an American to be CEO but he was worthless in the oil games played in Siberia. Al knew they would be sold off and any addition of new oil to their reserves would be welcomed. Upon arrival at the airport Al noticed the translator talking to a very nicely dressed older Russian lady. He told Al that she was one of the company's accountants coming back from Moscow and she needed a ride home, could we share our ride with her. Al agreed. He recognized her as he had seen her talking to Henry.

Al debriefed Paul about the trip to Moscow and told him of the plan for five new wells. Paul approved and asked if the Boss had approved. Al told him that he hadn't told the boss and Paul smiled and said that was the right thing to do because the Boss had too much on his plate and there was no need to bother him.

Henry requested a meeting with Al in the presence of Sergi. Sergi was Henry's ace in the hole. The company needed a president and Henry had recruited his friend Sergi. Sergi was a full colonel in the Russian Army but he was also in the military intelligence GRU. He was fairly fluent in English and he was also a gentleman. In the meeting Henry challenged Al on his drilling plan and stated that it was impossible to meet and we shouldn't make goals that are unrealistic. Al went over each line on the plan and questioned Henry why he thought it was impossible. After five hours Henry threw in all into Sergi's hands and voiced his objection in a rather weak manner. Al had won the battle as it was obvious that they had already talked with the Boss and he had already given his blessings. Al left the meeting determined to learn about the friendship between Henry and Sergi. Sergi was a proud Russian and a good leader, why did he need a friend like Henry. Surely he knew how Henry extorted his Russian drilling contractors, surely he knew how Henry womanized at work, and surely he knew all of it including Al's military record. Al had learned during his working in the Russian Far East that Moscow had a file with Al's name on it. Al had spent duty in the military intelligence and was a Russian specialist. He had learned more about the Russian military than he could ever forget but more importantly Al had worked for big brother and his name was on the Manwidth list. Manwidth is the unknown place in England that remains the most secret place on Earth. Yes Sergi knew who Al was or who Al had been and who Al had worked for. Al suspected that Sergi would never share this information with Henry as a matter of code of conduct from one old soldier to another. Al was correct and during his stay in Siberia Al and Sergi became friends. One day Sergi asked Al if it ever got to hot in Texas to work or play. Al said no, if it's too hot we go to the pond, river or the beach and fish. Sergi said that he had lived all his life in Siberia and it never got too cold for him to work, train or play. He didn't understand Russians from Moscow demanding to stop work when it gets cold. Al told him that he didn't think New Yorkers could live in Houston without air conditioners but his grandparents had lived there all his life and never had an air conditioner.

Al's translator had become disgruntled and bored, so he was given the duty of translating all shipping manifest. He was told that the new drilling program must be fully supported with materials. The translator was not happy about his new work assignment and started to avoid Al. The restaurant at the government hotel served a very fixed menu but the translator had been able to order off menu for Al. Now that the translator wasn't happy he started skipping meals. Al sensed his unhappiness so he decided to explain just how important the dam shipping manifest was to completing the overall plan. Not exciting work but absolutely necessary work if they were to be successful. After a bottle of vodka and eating at a new restaurant at Al's expense the translator warmed up to the idea of working. It was during the translator thaw that Al discovered his real character. One of his grandfathers had died in a gulag in the Far East. His other grandfather had been a Army general in the Russian army, so he had seen the best and worst of the communist. He confessed that he was recruited and had joined the communist party during his senior year of college and had been recognized for his language skills. It seemed that his main fear was of the bands of gypsies that roved near his summer home outside of St Petersburg. The gypsies had stolen his motor bike that his grandfather had given him for his 12th birthday and he could never either understand or forgive the dam gypsies. Al did like the translator but the translator would not let Al out of his sight even for one minute. He would escort Al to and from his hotel room and would always be nearby even during smoke breaks at work. It seemed to be against his nature to watch Al so close but something he had been told to do. Al would soon learn why.

The government restaurant food was down to beet soup and they decided to walk around town to find anywhere else to eat or maybe just go to a grocery store and purchase some food. Much to their surprise they found a kiosk that served hot roasted chicken. They also found a fish and sausage shop that had good stock and good prices. As Al was waiting at the kiosk and the translator was shopping in the fish shop, Al heard a voice. The weather was more than 30 deg below and most of the street was empty so it seemed so strange to hear a strange English voice. Al looked and saw no one except an apparent reindeer herder that was standing a few feet away. Al looked at him but he offered no eye contact. Al turned back towards the kiosk and again he heard "It's been 27 years". Al looked back and heard it again, "It's been 27 long years" and this time the man made eye contact. Al was totally shocked to be looking into the eyes of an old friend from the Agency days. During Al's last days in the Army the Agency had came recruiting and even though Al had been assigned to the Agency, he considered himself on Army duty. The man he was looking at served with him for two years and Al knew that he was recruited by the Agency. Al had known his wife, his son and had spoken to his brother once in Hawaii. It had been his brother the policeman who had told Al about him being recruited by the Agency. His name was Cornell; he was from Hawaii and had been in the Manhoonie squad. During war games they played the Viet Cong together. Al always volunteered to be a Viet Cong so he could raid the food pantries of the other side. Free cigarettes and C rations. What to hell was Cornell doing here in the middle of Siberia in a town of no where? Al was certain from Cornell's actions that they were being watched, so he only looked at him and nodded as the translator walked back to the kiosk. Then Al said very loud "yes it's been 27 dam years and the last time was on the Czech border." The translator looked stunned and said "what". Al said that the last time he had ate roasted chicken was when he was in Germany along the Czech border. Cornell smiled and walked away, stumbling like a drunk as he went on down the street.

Al was standing in front of the hotel when he noticed a large lady in her middle years pushing a very large baby stroller. She was dressed in warm clothes that had probably been purchased locally. Al helped her lift the baby carriage up the steps to the hotel entrance and she said Thank you in English. Al looked down into the baby carriage and saw a very fat and healthy blue eyed baby girl. She was wrapped in a pink blanket and her eyes said she was not too hot or too cold. Al asked the lady where she was from and she said Pennsylvania. Al looked at the baby and spoke to her. He said "you poor child, your new mother is going to take you back to Pennsylvania and teach you how to speak that GOD awful Pennsylvania Dutch language. The lady looked at Al then down at the baby and said, "Yes I am." Al could see the bond of love that was already established and ask her how she was doing. She told Al that the mafia was still trying to get more money from them but her husband was taking care of it. Her husband came up and introduced himself and told Al that he couldn't believe that the mafia knew exactly how much money they had in their bank account in Pennsylvania; He felt fortunate that they did not know about all his accounts. Al looked down at the baby and told them both that it looked like it was worth all their efforts and money. He knew it was. This was one lucky baby and she seemed to know it. This story would have a happy ending.

The next night Al slipped out of the hotel and went back to the kiosk hoping to find Cornell but he was no where to be found and in half an hour the translator found Al. He was very upset about Al leaving the hotel without telling him. The next night Al began exploring the town with the translator, every night after work they would walk the streets for a couple of hours or until they were dam near frozen. They never found Cornell but one of their best late night discoveries were the twin girls from Tomsk. They were beauty shop operators/ deluxe hair cutters and each weighed about 150 pounds.

They were big, blond and beautiful and identical twins. Only the color of their lipstick was different. One preferred orange and one red. Thanks to the twins and their gracious hospitality, Al and the translator finally bonded during biweekly hair cuts. The translator excelled using Al's humor with the girls. Al always insisted that the girls know that the translator's hair cut should remind them of his first day in school. Al told them that his hair cut should remind them of his first day in jail. They loved to hear this unusual American make jokes. They especially liked his Polish jokes. No pretense of conspiracy, just two men and two women in the land of the sunshine and silver snow. No words were ever spoken about Cornell to anyone but at least now Al knew what he was not supposed to see and why the translator wouldn't let him out of his sight. Al started making plans to find and attempt a rescue Cornell or at least talk to him.

The drilling program began and Henry and company started sabotaging the wells. If Paul had not been willing to check every detail of the well completions, Henry might have been successful. Henry's specialty was determining the place and size of explosives to be used during the fracturing of the well. Paul did not offer advice but he did check every detail of Henry's operations. After the third well had been fractured and proven to be less than commercial. Paul expected a thousand barrels a day well, and results proved to be twenty five barrels a day actual flow. Paul suddenly appeared to be smiling more than necessary. He discovered that the explosives had not been placed in the pay zone. Henry had set his explosives just above the pay zone and Paul had the numbers to prove it. This had happened on the last three wells and Henry had hung himself. Paul made a trip to Moscow to tell the Boss and to plan a side track drilling plan and possible recovery. Al remained in Siberia and Paul came back with a new drilling manager. Paul and Al had suspected that Henry was part of a bigger conspiracy but if so the Boss would handle it. The new drilling manager was a home office dick weed and not long on experience. Most of his career had been spent in West Texas in one field but it didn't matter because the boss didn't fire Henry. He moved him down in the organization and made sure he was fully exposed in all his dealings. The Boss told Al and Paul that he was getting pressure to sell part of the concession and he wanted to make sure we had proven reserves before the sale. The drilling program was adjusted to the new plan and results were immediate. The thousand barrels a day wells were pumping twenty five hundred BPD and Paul thought that we were only drilling the flanks of the main reservoir. Jim thought the same but was worried about water break through in the wells. The Boss got his wish and emphasis turned to getting the new oil to market.

After Henry was neutered by the Boss his main squeeze the blond Cossack warmed up to Al. She stayed late when Al worked late and gave him a ride back to the hotel. Her English was excellent but she seemed distant and never appeared to be sexually forward. She could drive her old two wheel drive Lauda in the snow and ice with little problems with the icy hills and turns. One day she brought some pictures to show Al. The pictures were of her parents and grand parents and the pictures reminded Al of his own family pictures. They appeared to be proud and fierce people. She also told Al of her Aunt running away with a reindeer herder and how the family struggled to bring her back. Finally she told Al of how her family had been deported to Siberia with only the clothes on their back. They had built log cabins and learned to live off the land. All medicine and food had to come from the land and in the early days most of the people in Siberia were exactly like her own family. Stalin's purges was not designed to populate Siberia, they were designed to rid the rest of Russia of undesirable or politically incorrect people. Al spoke to her about Cornell and she offered her help. No swearing to secrecy, no promises of pay, and no favors asked. She promised to help. Her connections with the post office would be her starting place and in a matter of days she had located Cornell. She arranged a meeting at a small Cossack restaurant on a Sunday afternoon. The translator wasn't present because he was sent to tour the Siberian oil museum and he seemed relaxed because Al was with the Cossack.

The place was empty and she and Al had ordered food and drink before Cornell showed up. Al told Cornell he wanted to help him get home and he would arrange for his truck and train fare into Kazakhstan and there he would join up with some oil company people that Al knew. He would hire on a laborer and work until it was time for his days off, then he would fly to Cyprus where he would report to the American embassy. Cornell ask Al why he was helping and Al told him that he was helping only because he knew his wife was from Ft. Worth and surely he wanted to see his son. Al said he had no political reasons and no obligations other than just an old friend and one human to another. Cornel asked if Al had remembered his feeling towards Sigmund Ree, the man who had been President of Korea during the Korean War. Al remembered because it was the only time he had seen hate in Cornell. Cornell was a soldier just like Al had been and both knew that hate got good men killed; hate was not allowed in soldiers, you must learn to fight and kill or be killed without hate. Al clearly remembered Cornell's hate of Sigmund Ree, The former President of Korea. Seems he had been friends of Cornels family and after the Korean War he left Korea then he had lived out his rich life style in the tropical paradise of Hawaii. Cornell could never understand a man who didn't love his country and especially a fellow Korean. Al said yes he remembered. Cornel asked Al what he thought of Russia and the Russian people. Al responded that he though they were the same as American people and only the Europeans had caused the cold war. They had started the cold war to keep Europe from becoming colonies of America or Russia. Communism and capitalism styles of government were both becoming failures for the same reasons but either sure as hell beat bowing to anyone calling themselves royalty. Cornell smiled and told Al that it was so good to see him, he told Al that if he needed anything while he was working in Russia to send him word. He told Al he had defected to Russia. In order to save their face the Agency had listed him as missing. He thought it better if he remained missing. They finished eating their reindeer and beet soup. Al thought it never tasted as good as when two old friends were sharing. Al looked at the Cossack and seemed puzzled why her beautiful blue eyes were the source of the tears running down her face. She must be thinking how stupid these Americans are. The drilling season had yielded fantastic results. New oil was increased three fold and even Houston seemed happy. Jim and Paul had both been correct in their guesses about the location of new oil but Paul had guessed best because the new oil he predicted had been across the river from the pipelines and trunk lines to market. The new oil Paul found must be trucked from the well site across the ice bridges and this meant they would only be able to sell six months of production and Russian oil trucks were hard to find. Jim's guesses were close to the production facilities and it would be easy to get his oil to market through the existing facilities once they had been expanded. Even Henry had been surprised by the success with new oil and Henry's new training seemed to be paying off.

Oil Patch Party

Working in Siberia had its ups and downs but the one constant was its always cold in Siberia. The drillers had accomplished more this year than Al had planned, the geologist had been nervously optimistic and production results were more than the Boss expected, more than Houston had dreamed of but after a colder than usual winter everyone was tired to the bone. Too tired too fight, too tired to argue, too tired to get vodka drunk and too tired to chase women. All emails had become terse and all meetings short and to the point. Everyone was ready to quit and go somewhere, anywhere except Siberia. The Russians dreamed of Black Sea resorts and sunshine, Henry dreamed of trucking thru Africa, the Boss dreamed of seeing his beloved Montana in the spring. Paul just dreamed; perhaps of his parents working for the Salvation Army in Indiana, standing in shopping centers ringing the bells. Al dreamed about his ranch and his cows and dog. That dog had been his friend since the day she crawled out of a basket full of her brothers and sisters and went home with Al. He knew all was ok because Raffel the semi legal Mexican was watching them if he wasn't in jail for the 4th DUI. He dreamed because he missed them and this extended stay away from home had not been easy.

The Boss decided we all needed a party. Sergei, the retired Russian Army officer made the arrangements. Times had been tough this winter for the locals, in spite of the extreme cold the Russian utility companies had been turning off heat and electricity for non payment. Homeless squatters had moved indoors in the unoccupied apartments and were staying warm by burning wood. No fireplaces in Russian apartments so they just opened windows for ventilation of their burning barrel. This created fire hazards in most buildings and calls to the police from all the buildings. The police knew that any evictions meant someone would freeze to death and they didn't do evictions. Food had also been scarce as the sugar beets and potato stashes dwindled. No reindeer meat available because all the herds moved south. Occasionally a truck load of frozen fish appeared and no one cared what kind of fish it was or where it came from. The boss arranged for an air freight shipment of food from the states, Sergei and company handled the paper work and finally the day came for the feast of champions. There would be enough turkey and ham for everyone to eat until they passed out.

The party was booked in an old restaurant in the middle of town. Instructions were given that all management would attend and they would all be on their best behavior. The old restaurant had seen its better days and had recently changed its seating arrangements to include private booths along the wall complete with curtains so the public could not look thru the windows and see who was dining. It seemed that anyone who had enough money to dine in private was normally connected to the Russian mafia or a corrupted public official. The booths kept the restaurant in business.

The seating arrangements were at a long table facing the door and were predetermined to make sure the best behavior was possible. Each setting had a name card. All walked in and sat at their designated place with the boss at the head of he table and Sergei at his right hand. Al was seated at the left hand side of the table next the boss; Paul and Hendry were across from all and the other 10 people at their named places. A speech was made by the boss thanking each person for their hard work and contributions to the successful year. He noted that we still had a lot or works to do but he knew he had the right team to do anything. Sergei nodded as if to say "My team in war or peace".

The waiters had started serving vodka as soon as they were seated and it seemed everyone was just in a sipping mood. They were all served a delicious bowl of Russian Borsht soup. The famous red beet soup with a few chunks of unidentified meat floating in it and a swirl of mayonnaise floating of top. Al hate the sight, smell and taste of Borsht but he did as always by fishing around for the meat then spooning out the juice while trying to avoid the mayonnaise. Every Russian knew it was common practice to cook rat meat with Borsht and the Russians usually ate the mayonnaise and the beets, leaving the meat untouched. It was considered very bad manners to make mention of eating rat because no one was proud of it. As they finished the soup Al noticed that several of the team was missing, he thought just a trip to the bathroom or maybe having a private conversation.

The waiters brought out a roasted turkey and a baked ham and placed one in front of Sergei and one in front of the boss. They each cut off a small piece and fed it to the other with a fork. Al was really getting hungry just watching the ham and turkey being sliced. The front door of the restaurant opened and to Al's amazement a group of people was waiting as the boss and Sergei picked up the trays and handed the ham and turkey to the people outside. Al thought it must be some Russian tradition being followed. Al looked at Paul and Hendry and quietly asked "What to hell is going on. Hendry rolled his eyes and said nothing. Paul turned his head and said "It's a Russian thing". Anatoly the construction manager looked at Oleg the Engineering manager and said "What to hell is going on, these two are making love with food while we starve". Oleg looked at him and said "It's an American thing".

In rapid success the same process was repeated ten times. Al looked out the door and saw the crowd. It was Russian Orthodox priest, homeless people, some of the company workers, reindeer herders and a crowd of town people that filled the streets. Al saw Broom Hilda from the Orphanage. Al's favorite Russian and he visited her often to see what he could do to help her. The first time they met was when Al went with a friend to deliver some clothing. Al asked her what her biggest challenge was in providing for one hundred and fifty orphans. When she told Al she needed nothing from him for their day to day living but she felt bad because she could not keep records of their families. That ended with Al bringing her three computers and a service tech to teach her and her assistants how to use them. Of course there were the normal precautions on her part about who paid for them and if they were bugged. Every meeting with Broom Hilda was eventful but usually ended with Al learning a new Russian cuss word. He would always start out with saying "How is this communist crap working out, the country is going to hell in bread basket". She would get mad and say "It's not communism; it is lazy, stupid people in the government that aren't doing their job". After a few visits Broom Hilda knew Al started the fight with her because when he saw the orphans in their hand me down, patched and faded clothes, he usually cried. Sometimes the translator refused to translate Al's or Broom Hilda's words but they came to know, respect and love each other and she knew that if she made a request to Al it would be done. Al knew she was the mother for 150 kids, and she also didn't use excuses. She smiled at Al as if she just knew he had something to do with the free food. She was wrong. Al felt better with the food distribution process as it was obviously a sign of good will but in strange fashion and Al thought "how many hams and turkeys did they order"? He later learned it was 150 hams and turkeys. When he saw Broom Hilda he always felt that she knew about his responsibility for the Catholic priest disappearance and a feeling of guilt and shame overcame him. The Russian law states that only orphans with disabilities that were not treatable were available for overseas adoption. The priest had learned how to subvert the law by having some low level government employee sign off to some phony handicap allowing perfectly healthy kids be sold into adoption to foreign parents. The price for adoption was twenty five thousand and after paying off the mafia handlers, the priest used the money to build churches. Warnings were given and several of the new churches were bulldozed to the ground for lack of proper building permits but money talks and finally the priest died. Al would view it as suicide. Al truly believed that people were God's greatest creations, not sticks and stones called churches that were created with the blood of children and corrupt government employees. Somehow Broom Hilda knew Al's beliefs and his courage to right some wrong, perhaps she knew because it was also her beliefs. Their show of love and affection to each other would always start out with "How's this commie crap working out for you?" then each learning a few new cuss words.

Al looked up he saw along legged redhead talking to Paul. He got up and left with her, then Henry was approached by a blue eyed brunet and he left with her. What to hell was going on he thought? Then Al noticed he was alone at the table except for the boss and Sergei. A pleasantly endowed blond lady walked over to Al and said "please come with me". Al had seen this girl before and remembered her because she worked at the barber shop/beauty salon and had an identical twin sister. They always wore different color lipstick to confuse the customers and liven up things. They were from the Tyumen region of Russia and were referred to as the Tyumen twins. Al's translator told one of the twins liked him. Al thought back to his first hair cut. The translator was in the barber chair next to Al and one of the twins ask Al what kind of hair cut he wanted. Al told her to make the translators hair look like his first day in high school and to make my hair look like my first day in jail. One of the twins laughed and one looked shocked. Dam translator never told Al which one liked him because he said he couldn't tell the difference. Al followed her. She walked over and pulled the curtain to open the private booths. The booths had been converted from chairs and table to a bed. Al thought that the only this could get better would be for the other twin to show up. The room had a boom box and the first thing Blondie did was to start the music. Al thought it strange that the boom box started playing Al's favorite Jim Reeves music but in Al's head there was a song playing from the movie Oh Brother Where Art Thou. "Go to sleep little baby, go to sleep little baby, just you and me and the devil makes three, go to sleep little baby". He had noticed while walking by the other booths that each one had a different music. Al smiled and thought that it must be Hendry listening to Gordon Lightfoot and Paul listening to the Eagles, Probably Jim the Geologist listening to the strings of Bach. How funny this evening had turned out and when Blondie touched him he forgot all about ham and turkey.

The next morning the boss came into Al's office asking "Did you enjoy the party?"

He explained that he ordered the party food and he caught hell from Houston. So he paid for everything himself but even the town mayor got upset because he had planned a party during such hard times, He promised the mayor he could have the leftovers, then Sergei made sure everyone in town knew there would be lots of leftovers. The "guest" was an idea from him and Sergei, said he chose Blondie as Al's guest because his translator told him that that was the only girl in town that he had looked at twice. Al had no comment until the boss ask him if he got his moneys worth and he responded with "and a lot more" but I am still hungry.

Now that they had tons of new oil it meant almost nothing unless they could get it to market. Fortunately Henry's new boss had discovered Russian women and Henry was back more and more of the day to day decision making. The new boss was happily married back in Texas but Siberia was a long way from Texas and it was cold and lonely in Siberia. The translator had become the new bosses friend and Al suspected that he needed the translators help for romantic reasons. Al had seen the new boss entertaining a lady and her family who worked in government relations. Al also noticed he had been entertaining them on his company credit card. Al knew the company had a dozen bean counters in Houston who lived for the moment they could find wrong in his expense reports. Over the next few months the new boss seemed to spend more and more time doing elaborate emails back to Houston concerning his expense reports. Al thought it was time to make Henry a hero.

Al invited Paul and Henry to diner. Surprisingly the Boss had found his way to Siberia and he and Sergi had joined Al and Henry for diner. They started the diner with vodka toast to the new found oil, spoke about Yukos oil company problems and had more vodka. With diner they had Russian beer and wine. Henry became livid about the new oil and no way to get it to market. After a few minutes Al told them that recently he had read that Russian oil men had pioneered the drilling of horizontal oil wells and asked in Henry had ever drilled one. Al knew that Henry had drilled horizontal wells and he also knew they were failures. He also knew that the failure was because of the oil bearing formations. Henry boasted that he could drill horizontal wells but the ones he had drilled had not yielded good results. Al then proposed that by drilling a horizontal well under the rivers they could use the well pipe casings as a pipeline for the new oil. Henry's eyes lit up and he guaranteed the Boss and Sergi that it could be done. This would make Henry a hero and it would be a solution to the growing Yukos legal problems. Sergei promised to get permits and the boss said he would make sure the production facilities would get increased to accommodate the new oil. Al thought it was amazing how a couple bottles of vodka, a case of beer and a few liters of wine had produced such clear results and commitment. Maybe his old boss had been correct when he told Al to never trust anyone unless he had gotten drunk with them. By the time the ice bridges had melted and spring run off had finished they were pumping new oil under the mighty Ob River.

Houston was so pleased with the new results and improved production they decided to fire Henry, sell the entire operation and force the Boss and Paul to retire. Al came home when the boss retired to check of Raffel and the farm. Al went in for his yearly health check up and some rest. Siberia had been hard money and yes the doctors found something.

CHAPTER 8

2004 COUNTY ROAD 49

The retirement farm that Al had bought with his Russian money seemed to be a good investment. CR 49 had been a dope smugglers heaven because it had its own airport and one of the main power distribution lines from the nuke plant running into the electric starved Houston. After months of land clearing and fence building Al had finally bought some cows. The dope smuggling operations had gone belly up after the owner of the airport turned up murdered and his body was found six months later after the coyotes and small varmints had reduced it to a skeleton.

Al had watched the dope drops and how the small airplane could take off vertically and zoom down the power line at incredible speeds. No DEA plane could catch it and no radar could track it when it went down the power lines. The field of energy given off by the power lines would block all traces. These dope smugglers were good, very good. Seems the airport owner had been working with both the DEA and the local police. Al could track the exit of the plane and know that it was heading straight out into the Gulf of Mexico and down to Central America. The high speeds and the vertical landing and take offs made it impossible to catch. So the DEA in their black unmarked helicopter watched Al and his wife cleared and burned marijuana plants and ploughed under up the magic mushrooms. The black helicopter would hover 20 or 30 feet above the ground just waiting to see if there was an attempt to harvest. The good guys had no chance to catch the plane and the real drug dealers but shortly after the black helicopters appearance the body of the airport owner was found in the back of the farm.

The airport was up for sale and it was bought from the bank by a high school drop out from Florida who had built his own P-51 Mustang. He owned all the world records except one for P-51 speeds and altitudes. Exxon sponsored him and paid him well to set world records. Bruce was born to fly and made a daily practice of flying high fast and crazy. Every day he practiced landing without his engine running. Bruce was an interesting character but CR49 had others and he provided all with daily air shows. He still sold fuel to the dope dealers but allowed no drops or pickups by dopers cars or in most cases a fed ex truck. Every day he took up his P-51 looking for the Red Barron and the Japs bombing Pearl Harbor.

CR49 historian was Jess. He owned 20 acres and loved to buy and sell small animals. His 20 acres could have been a petting zoo. He preferred to buy old and sick animals from the local cattle auction and feed them with mounds of day old bread and expensive sweet feed. He nursed them back to good health and then sold them and started over. He tried to appear like a cold hearted animal trader but he loved animals and since his retirement as an electrician it had become his full time job. The only thing out of place on Jess's 20 acres was a couple of dog runs. Dog runs that looked like a gray hound race track. Occasionally he had gray hounds that he was nursing back to good health and it had the appearances of an animal humane effort but appearances are only skin deep. In truth Jess owned more than 50 racing gray hounds at race tracks from Florida to California. He had been raising gray hounds since he was a teenager. His father was poor and ran a vegetable stand for a living. Jess hated the vegetable stand because it denied him from being a baseball player that he could have been. He could not play sports because he was made to work the vegetable stand when he was not in school. When he was out buying vegetables for his father Jess had discovered an illegal gray hound race track in a black community near Austin. It was the kind of race track that used live rabbits and raced only two dogs at a time. He hung around the track until he learned the business of dog raising, racing and gambling. In the back roads dog tracks there were no photo finishes, close races usually ended with the judges bare knuckle fighting and the rabbit was always skinned and cooked into rabbit stew. Jess got into the business when a dog handler who was moving racing gray hounds from Florida to Arizona had stopped to spend the night and make some small change with his ringers. He had a dog with great blood lines but who was nearing the end of his racing days and he gave him to Jess and told the dog's owners the dog had became crippled. Jess nursed the dog back to good health and took the dog to the match races. Good handling and good diet allowed the old dog to win a young Jess a lot of money. Forty years later the blood line of the old dog was still winning races and Jess was still making money. He had been recognized as breeder of the year several times and his dogs had won the big races. Few people knew about the old man or his dogs. He made so much money that he had to hide some of it and sick animals was a good way to hide money if you had the best CPA in the county filing taxes. No one paid much attention to an old man nursing sick dogs and animals back to good health. Even the dope dealers paid no attention to Jess but he paid attention to them and when the owner of the airport disappeared Jess was sure that he was next to go because he knew all their dealings and he had seen all the players making the drop offs and pick ups. The road to the airport was a dirt road and from his tiny shack he could see it all. He also kept car license tag numbers. He also knew which law enforcement agencies were involved. Jess kept a gun in his pocket and hoped he would not have to use it but because CR 49 was remote he took weekly target practice so the dopers took notice of the old man who ran an animal orphanage shooting plastic milk jugs. He also carried a smaller gun in his pocket just in case. When he was involved in a car accident and was life flighted to Houston and knocked out of it for 3 days his wife was sure his body would be found later. The police had no record of the accident and they towed his wrecked truck. No trace of Jess for 3 days until he came to in the ICU and called his wife to come get him.

Joe had grown up in the barrios of East Houston. His grand father had started a small welding shop and Joe and his wife had grown it into a major fabrication plant. Joe's secret was he employed mostly family and first generation Mexicans. They had three teenage daughters and decided to move out of the city to a farm. His 300 acres was an old unproductive rice field and Joe knew absolutely nothing about animals or farming. Some of his first generation Mexicans knew how to build fences so Joe soon enclosed his three hundred acres and proceeded to buy cows. Joe paid top prices for old and sick cows at the local auction and soon became the source of contention to the normal cow buyers who bought and sold for slaughter companies. The first couple of years Joe lost a lot of cows, some just ran away and some died. Cow farmers aren't very good at taking advice and each one shows preference to different breeds. Joe didn't know one breed from others so Joe usually let his wife buy the cows. She seemed to know good mama cows and the cows improved because she looked for the obvious signs of good mama cows. The milk bags are a good place to judge mama cows. Eventually Joe admitted he was afraid of cows after one of his cows broke through the fence and ended up at Al's farm. Al put the cow in his corral and told Joe to come get his cow. The cow had no brand and several other nearby neighbors had claimed the cow but Al was suspect and even though the cow had no brand or markings indication it was Joe's cow, Joe had made pictures of each cow he had bought and the picture proved it was their cow. Joe showed up at Al's corral to pick up his cow with a home made trailer that Joe had fabricated himself. The trailer was small and well built but it looked more like a trailer for a vegetable stand than a cow trailer. Al had penned the cow with his 4 wheeler and determined that the horse he was so proud of was not effective at chasing cows, especially cows that loved to fight. Joe had a fighting cow and would charge anyone near her. After watching Joe and his brother in law trying to chase the cow into the trailer and having the cow chase them into the truck, Al decided to show Joe and his pencil thin mustached brother in law how to deal with fighting cows. He told Joe that he could not be a cowboy and be afraid of cows. The cows could sense the fear and would take advantage of it. Then Al proceeded to ram the cow with his 4 wheeler until the cow submitted and finally ran into the trailer. The brother in law looked at Al as if he were just another crazy white boy but he understood the message of fear. Joe's beginnings of being a cowboy had started and he would lean a good deal about cows. He allowed his wife to pick out all the mama cows and Al to pick out his bulls. Al started buying bulls for Joe after Joe came back from the auction barn with his new prized bull. Al and Jess pointed out to Joe that bulls normally have a set of nuts the size of pineapples and Joe's new bull was missing his nuts which meant he would not be fathering calves anytime soon. In a few years Joe's cows were among the best on CR 49. Joe also took note of the dope dealers and carried a gun at all times. A policeman friend had taught him how to shoot and Al had no reservations that this guy who had called the barrio home most of his life would defend himself and family and his cows.

Sam drove down Cr 49 once a month to see if anyone had scrap metal for sale. Sam was an old black preacher man who had a pleasant disposition and smiling, all knowing eyes. His voice was low but he spoke in clear English and always seemed happy to be there. The first time Al met Sam he noticed that his family name was one that Al recognized from his home town. Al also remembered that some of the best cowboys had the same name. Sam smiled and told Al that his family came from up there but he had been in the county more than fifty years. They quickly became friends. Sam was no ordinary man and especially no ordinary junk man. Al had made himself a promise that each time he saw a Cross on a Church he would say Thank You GOD, Amen. Sam was a Preacher and Al had said many "Thank You GOD" to Sam's Church cross. The Church had been there as long as Al could remember but he never told Sam of his promise. Sam's visits became often and Al learned to listen because Sam used Al's judgments when he was confused. Sam was eighty five years old when they met and ten years later he was still telling everyone that he was eighty five. One day he asked Al's opinion on a legal matter. Seemed that a man and a woman in his Church and given rat poison to the woman's husband and after he became deathly ill they carried him to a clinic that was more than a hundred miles away. After the husband died they confessed it all to Sam and he wanted to know if he should violate the sanctity of his ministry. Al told him that the guilt and final judgment would seem to suffice and they agreed. Over the years they would bump into each other at various places and both families seemed confused as to how they became friends and neither seemed to mind the indifference of their families. When Al was driving himself to Chemo treatments Sam would mysteriously appear standing beside the road waiting for a ride. Al received Sam's best sermons during these rides and Sam seemed to just appear and disappear at the right times.

Developers had moved into Sam's neighborhood and Sam was a millionaire but his demeanor never changed. He remained eighty five years old and he always showed up when Al really needed a perspective on his battles with life and death.

One day Al told Sam that his neighbor had some scrap metal and Sam went to talk to the man. He returned and told Al he would not deal with the man because of one of his previous experiences with people he didn't like or trust. Seems a farmer had an old rice combine and told Sam he could have it for scrap. Sam went to the man's farm and proceeded to use a cutting torch to cut up a combine which just happened to be parked where he had shown Sam the old combine. A couple of hundred thousand dollar combine sold as scrap metal. Sam did three months in jail for his mistake. He didn't put a time line on the story so the price could have been less but Sam's memory of jail was no less. He was the only preacher that Al had met that paid regular visits to the jails to talk to people. When Al told Sam of the dope dealers and all the neighbors carrying guns Sam did something that made them go away but he never told Al what he did. About a mile from his Church was the remains of an old beer joint that had been a source of contention because of its proximity to Sam's Church. The happiest day of Sam's recent memory was when the new land owner decided to tear down the old beer joint and let Sam drive the dozer through the building. Sam could not get his drivers license renewed so Al drove him to the Dozer and remembered the look on his face and the shinning in his old brown eyes as he leveled the place. Al remembered Sam's smile that said "I am tearing down a piece of Hell."

The dope dealers gave up and moved out and CR 49 became a show place of good quality animals and friendly neighbors. Al thought it so funny how a fabricator, a dog breeder and a crazy fly boy who would have loved to have done air battle with the Red Barron would bond together and help deliver baby calves during the cold rainy winters. The fifth year after the dope dealers had moved CR 49 produces 4 of the 10 champion breeds of cows at the county fair. Incredible that a road only 5 miles long and zero political connections could walk away with the honors considering in happened in the county that produced some of the best beef cows in the world and competed against places that had thousand of cows and hundreds of thousand acre ranches. A dog breeder, a retired engineer, a crazed fly boy and a third generation Mexican welder had made the big boys take notice. These guys didn't do things the old way. They did things their way in spite of the well connected drug dealers and the torrid gulf coast weather. The barns, fences, roads, buildings, cows and grasses were all different but the heart and soul of it all was the same. Their only threat could come from the Houston developers who had pumped the price of farm land to twenty five thousand an acre but CR 49 would remain a pocket of farms surrounded by million dollar homes. Most folks would say it makes no sense to stay on this expensive land and raise cows for show but to these guys it did. They all wanted to spend the remainder of their lives doing exactly what they were doing. They all fully expected their children to sell to developers after their deaths and spend the money living well but DNA is a funny but very predictable thing.

CHAPTER 9

1994 "CHRISTIE"

Ester was the daughter of an Apache Indian from Mexico. Her father was a rancher and had accumulated a considerable plot of land in Mexico. The land was barren, little rain and always hot. Life was always tough and the starvation of even one of his cows was cause for alarm. Most of his winters were spent burning the sharp needles from cactus so his cows could eat them and survive the barren land. One of Ester's six brothers came to Texas, found permanent work and was soon joined by the other brothers and sisters. They lived in Texas for the remainder of their lives. Ester was unusual in that she was very beautiful but was closely guarded by her brothers. After their mother died her father joined the children in Texas and lived with Ester. The brothers worked at different companies and started several small successful businesses. They were proud people and the brothers were not happy when Ester fell in love with a Cuban. After Ester became pregnant the Cuban disappeared and it was thought that the brothers had made him leave. It was never clear where the leaving was to go this world or on to the other.

Ester gave birth to a daughter who was also beautiful, tall, and straight as an arrow. She showed few resemblances to her mothers Apache blood but she had uncommon beauty. She was full of life and Ester delighted in her daughter and often worked two jobs to make sure she could provide well for her child. When Christie was eighteen years old she enrolled in the University of Texas and moved to Austin. She started studying medicine and had very good grades until she met a young man named Michael. Michael was just plain no good. He had been an only child and was raised entirely by his mother and mostly on the monthly welfare checks his mother received. He never knew who his father was and showed little if any respect for anyone. He was not big enough to be an athletic even if his mother had allowed it. His mother hand sewed most of his clothes until he was almost in high school, then she made sure he had the latest sneakers and expensive clothes. He was not popular with the other boys but all the girls liked him. Something about his good looks and effeminate side made the girls feel comfortable but he never seemed satisfied with one girlfriend and the girls didn't seem to mind sharing him and his affections. He became a ladies man and it seemed that the girls always paid his way whether it was to the movies, a dance or even the cars they cruised around in. Michael paid nothing because he had nothing to pay with. He never had a job or even wanted one. Mother was always there to help until her cancer made it impossible to provide for him. After his mothers death he moved to Austin with one of his girlfriends and the town seemed to be made for him. Austin had many good looking girls to provide his needs and he always had a nice place to live. He lived with whoever could tolerate him.

Christie met Michael in a bar on 6ᵗʰ street and they became friends and lovers. Christie's grades started to drop and soon she was telling her mother that she wanted to drop out of the university for a semester. Michael had an addiction to cocaine and he had introduced Christie to the drug. Most of the drugs were provided by Michael's girlfriends but he had met the providers of the drugs and had befriended them. They liked him because he seemed to be a magnet for girls. The pushers had also taught him to sell drugs. He was small time seller and small time user. Michael did not want to lose his good looks to drugs and his habit never seemed to increase but most of the girls that he sold drugs to always wanted more. Christie was no exception. By the time Ester knew that her daughter had a drug habit she was already a major user. Ester called a family meeting with her brothers and told them of the problem, she also told her boy friend Paul Ed. Paul Ed was her only boy friend and marriage between them was never mentioned. None of her brothers knew she had a boy friend but Paul Ed was no ordinary boy friend. He spoke fluent Spanish because he was raised on a ranch in South Texas where all the ranch hands spoke Spanish. His family was actually Jewish and although not very religious they still observed the traditional holidays of the Jews. Paul Ed had lied about his age and joined the navy when he was sixteen years old. The navy had made him a diver and the day he made a dive out of a submarine under the ice changed his life forever. The dive master had miscalculated the water depth and Paul Ed had suffered major damage to his ear drum. He spent months in a Navy hospital and it was there they discovered that he was under age they discharged him from the Navy. He went home to South Texas to work on the ranch. He stayed there until he was eighteen years old and then he joined the Army. He rose to the rank of major and spent most of his time with the Special Forces. During an assignment in Panama he was assigned to a DEA task force with the job of stopping drugs from entering the USA from Panama. When he learned that some US Army soldiers were involved in the drug smuggling Paul Ed became a one man show. He tortured the soldiers involved and was determined to learn all the connections of the US Army.

After one of his interrogations got out of hand he was retired from the Army. Some of his associated were charged with crimes but the Army and the government did not want Paul Ed to go to trial. He was retired and for the next two years he was a fundraiser for the legal expenses of his colleagues. Eventually Paul Ed was redeemed when Panama was invaded by US forces and the president of Panama was captured and brought to the US and convicted for drug smuggling. Paul Ed believed the level of involvement was President to President.

Ester's brothers had determined that rehab was best for Christie and they enrolled her in the best rehab program affordable. Paul Ed had other plans. He often visited Al's ranch and they talked about the old days in the Agency. Late in March Paul Ed told Al of his plan for the redemption of his girlfriend's daughter. Ester had suffered greatly because of the ongoing rehab and the brothers always mentioned the Cuban and her poor choices for a father. Al joked that Paul Ed was upset because the drug dealers had upset his sex life and he just wanted an adventure but Al knew Paul Ed very well and he never thought twice about Paul Ed not getting his redemption with the dealers.

Whenever Raffel would see Paul Ed's truck parked on Al's ranch he would always come up to practice his Spanish. Al never interfered with or added to their conversations. When Al had bull calves to be castrated he always let Raffel do it. His magic knife worked wonders of turning bull calves into steers. Paul Ed was also good with knives but Raffel knew how to cut with out spilling a lot of blood or doing damage to the cows. Raffel could nurse the sickest cows back to good health and he seemed enjoyed doing it. He detested Al using drugs on the sick cows, so Al usually relented and let Raffel nurse the cows back to good health. Paul Ed seemed to understand Raffel and it came as a surprise to Al when Paul Ed asked them if they wanted to go to Austin with him. Both agreed and the next morning Paul Ed picked them up.

On the drive to Austin Al questioned Paul Ed as to why he wanted to visit Austin? Paul Ed said he needed some information that he could only get in Austin.

The Hilton hotel at the end of 6th street must have thought that Paul Ed Al and Raffel were a new music group because they paid no attention to their cowboy dress or the fact that their only luggage was an ice chest full of beer when they checked in.

After checking into the hotel Al proceeded to take a nap, Raffel headed to the closest bar and Paul Ed walked over to the state capitol building to visit an old friend from South Texas. When Paul Ed returned he and Al went to find Raffel. It wasn't too far because Raffel had made some new friends and had lever left his original bar stool. He was not drunk but getting drunk was his plan as soon as he learned why Paul Ed had wanted him to come to Austin. They left the bar and walked down to 5th street and had diner at a Mexican restaurant. Paul Ed told them why he came to Austin. He wanted to meet Christie's boyfriend and drug provider named Michael. After finishing diner they walked back to 6th street and down to the club Picasso. After being seated and ordering drinks Al noticed Paul Ed looking around to locate his prey. Obviously he had received some information from his friend in the capitol building. Al asked the waitress if they had Canadian Classic whiskey and she said yes. Al ordered a triple shot and took notice that Raffel didn't need another beer because he was still sipping the first one. Paul Ed had not touched his drink and he seemed to be memorizing everything about everybody at the table with Michael. Al noticed several good lookers with Michael and he also noticed that Michael had eye lashes like a woman and his face seemed to be full of soft lines and he definitely looked effeminate. One of the good lookers looked at Al and he gave a wink, to which she responded by smiling and looking away towards Michael. Al thought that a hundred dollar hooker always looks good but that was the old days and now with all this inflation crap she probably wants five hundred an hour. He thought that he could probably get five hundred worth of enjoyment but the price of his calves was only five hundred dollars and what man in his right mind would trade a year old calve for an hour with a hooker. He never gave it another thought because Paul Ed had asked if they were ready to leave. Al paid the bill and he noticed that the prey was on the move, he also noticed that the conversation in Spanish between Paul Ed and Raffel was very pointed and very direct.

Outside the bar they waited for Michael to come out and say good night to his girls. His girls headed to their working bars looking for customers. Raffel approached Michael and ask if he spoke Spanish. He said no so Raffel spoke in English but with a

Spanish accent that Al had never heard him use. He told him that he was new in town and he had a new source for coke. He wanted to make him a deal but only on a small time basis because he knew that Michael was friends with the Mexican mafia. He pointed to Al and Paul Ed and said they were his friends and money backers. They wanted to see how he operated before they made investment in him. He suggested they walk as they talk. Michael listened as they walked to the city lake. Once they had walked the three blocks to the lake Michael was very interested. He had set his own price which was about half of what he was paying the Mexican mafia and after Raffel told him that his product would be coming straight from Columbia and a much better product.

Michael seemed surprised when Paul Ed quickly handcuffed his right wrist. He offered no resistance because he thought he was being busted by undercover cops. He never carried drugs and had little money. He felt confident that it was just more harassment and certainly Michael was no stranger to police harassment. Paul Ed raised Michel's cuffed wrist over a low hanging branch of a tree and quickly cuffed his left hand. Both his hands over his head he quickly realized that these guys were not police but he had no idea what they wanted with him. Paul Ed quickly told him that he wanted to know the names and addresses of all his drug providers. His first thought that the balding fat man with steel blue eyes wanted the names of his providers so he could eliminate them and Michael seemed willing to provide anything he knew but he actually knew very little. He gave names and places when they hung out but he didn't know addresses or who they worked for or even who was in charge of providing his drugs. After Paul Ed was sure he had all the information he said something in Spanish to Raffel. Raffel reached out and loosened Michael's belt, he pulled down his jeans and underwear as if he was skinning a deer. Michael was frozen with fear when Raffel grabbed his scrotum to discover that Michael's balls had been sucked up into his body because of the fear. Raffel knew where to start fishing and soon he was holding Michaels balls in his hand. Quickly he cut the scrotum sack gently pulled one of the balls down. By this time Michael had fainted so Raffel took his time and asked Paul Ed to give him some light. Paul Ed held him pen light as Raffel continued his cutting. His sharp knife scrapped the cords from the balls and his careful cutting cause very little blood loss. The partial castration was over in less than three minutes.

Michael came to after Raffel had pulled up his underwear and jeans. As Raffel was fastening Michael's belt Paul Ed stepped forward and took the hand cuffs off. He spoke slow and direct. Make no mistake the oyster thing Paul Ed held in his hand was Michael's left ball. Paul Ed placed the ball in Michael's shirt pocket and told him he may want to keep it. Paul Ed showed it to him and told him to feel himself to see if one of his balls was really missing. Michael's went into his pants and as he felt for his missing ball he fainted. Raffel took his baseball hat dipped water from the lake and poured it on Michael. Paul Ed again started talking. He told Michael that the loss of one ball would not interfere with either his sex life of his masculinity if he had any. He had lost his left ball because of Christie. Paul Ed assured him that if the information he had provided was lies they would return and remove the right ball. Removal of his remaining ball would affect his sex life. Here is what he wanted. First of all Michael would get gainful employment. The next time they met he must have proof he had a job and had actually paid taxes. Secondly, if ever again there was another Christie he would lose his right ball.

The next day they left Austin and Paul Ed wanted to drive through bluebonnet country. They were now in bloom and any real Texas whether he comes from the woods of East Texas or the barren South Texas ranch country or even the far flat North Country, they all love the bluebonnets. Al never understood this but he also loved seeing the blue bonnets in bloom.

When they arrived back at Al's ranch Paul Ed told them that next month they would all go back to Austin. Al said that it would probably be miserably hot and Raffel said he would find a better

Mexican food restaurant. Paul Ed said thanks and he was going to see Ester and take her the blue bonnets that he had picked. Al told him he might still get arrested for picking bluebonnets. Raffel left riding the four-wheeler, looking for sick cows and Al sat down to talk to his Blue Heeler dog named Whoopee. Whoopee was half Australian Sheppard and half Catahoula. She was born without a tail and Al didn't want or need a dog but since the day he say her and a dozen of her brothers and sisters in a washtub at the local feed store they had been friends. She had crawled out of the wash tub and followed Al through the feed store; she had been following his ever move since that day. She was a cow dog and even as a puppy she was totally unafraid of cows and horses. She could out smart and out run them. She would spend hours herding the cows. Any strays were chased back to the herd. She would do this with Al watching. When Al quit paying attention she would lose interest and come to be petted by Al. When she was a puppy Al's grand children would let her join them for a ride on the four wheeler. Al thought that one of the most beautiful sights he had ever seen was his red headed grand daughter with her milk like complexion setting next to Whoopee. When she was a full grown seventy pound dog she still liked to ride but there was barely room for Al and Whoopee on the seat. Al and Whoopee had a lot to talk about. He needed to figure out a way to tell the old black preacher man Sam what had happened in Austin. He knew it would be a matter of days before Sam arrived. He knew Sam would arrive because Sam's son had won the Medal of Honor while serving in Vietnam and he was a good friend to Paul Ed. They served in the same unit and Sam's son had saved Paul Ed's life. He crawled more than a hundred yards under fire to save Paul Ed and he had been rewarded for his heroic efforts with a Medal of Honor. If anyone could talk sense into Paul Ed's head it would be Sam's son. Sam's son had just retired after serving thirty five years as an electrical inspector for the city of Houston. He was a walking encyclopedia for building codes. Remembering every code known to mankind had served to fight his demons of war. He was also a good man.

Al and Whoopee sat by the barn and listened to the old LP's of
Hank Sr and Jim Reeves and Al watched the Chicken Hawk framed
against a clear blue sky searching for a field mouse or a young rabbit
and Whoopee watched the cows graze. Next month would be here
way too soon and Al was making plans for the type of weapons
they would carry on their next trip to Austin. Surely Paul Ed didn't
intend to castrate the entire Mexican mafia. Al made a note to call
his cousin the cop who was working with the organized crime task
force and learn all he could about the Austin Mexican mafia. He also
made plans to have a barbeque for Ester. Ester and Al's wife were best
friends. He also made plans to visit a couple of her brothers. Al never
liked any of the brothers but they always treated Al with respect and
they liked Al. They seemed to distain the fact that Al had a lot of
Indian blood. The kind of Indian blood they feared more than they
feared any white man.

Al knew if he couldn't turn Paul Ed around their weekend trips
may take them into Mexico and maybe on to Columbia. Al told
Whoopee "I really think I am too dam old for this" but he knew he
couldn't say no to Paul. He had never been able to say no to Paul, not
in Laos, Burma, and Vietnam or even in Saudi. Suddenly he thought
about their time in Saudi. Paul always told the Saudi's that he was
Jewish and the Saudis still loved him. The Saudis that Paul Ed and
Al had dealt with were all high level royal family and they knew full
well that Al was a devout Christian who read his Bible daily and Paul
Ed was born and raised a Jew. Thank goodness the Saudis were not
involved in this mess or were they. Was it true that Columbian drug
money was being use to fund the fundamentalist Muslim preacher
that Al and Paul Ed had met in Saudi. Al thought he was already
dead but Paul Ed thought he was still hiding in Pakistan or back
in Saudi being hid by his family. Both Al and Paul Ed had mixed
feelings about this preacher because he had played a large role in
kicking the Russians out of the Middle East and he did come from
a pretty good family. These mixed emotions changed the day they
saw the world trade Center buildings fall but until then the preacher

had been killing the same dam Russians that had provided the guns that had been used to kill Americans in every war they had been involved in. Al thought that somewhere along the way the preacher had started believing his own bullshit and someone or something had taught him to hate Jews and Christians. Most likely it was the Americans and Britt's living in the Aramco housing compound in Dhahran. They seemed to lose all morals and consciousness when they arrived in Saudi to work for the oil companies. After another round of Hank and Jim Reeves music Al told Whoopee "I am really too dam old for this, I am going home and you are staying here to watch the cows".

Chapter 10

2010 "Never Felt Better"

The years passed and after following Paul Ed into Mexico for some Norco hunting Al had mellowed out. The boss had left him alone after his bout with cancer while he started his own oil company but kept in touch to learn if Al needed anything. Paul Ed changed after his wife and soul mate passed. He didn't come calling and even when he did his spirit had been broken. Al had retired to recover from Lung cancer and was watching his old dog grow older. Whoopee always listened but was too old to run her usual 10 miles. She preferred to just watch the cows. Al's retirement had turned into consulting. Ever so often he would get a call from some young VP from the oil company. He would spend a few months helping get everything organized and approved by the money boys, screening new people. The VP would eventually have enough confidence to stick to the plan and let his people do the work. It was always understood that Al would be watching over the reports to identify potential problems or down falls. Al usually did this from home with the latest and greatest software and a company computer. His mistake had been keeping his Blackberry phone active. The phone seems to allow people from work to call him at any time. This week had been a constant buzzing of the Blackberry coupled with CAT scan findings of some new bugs.

Al had stopped building fence, headed home to the computer for an on line meeting. He stopped at the local bowling alley for a burger. The gal cooking burgers knew how to do it right, she made a good burger. Al walked in the diner for his burger and was oblivious to all. He held the old blackberry deciding how to respond to the heads up before the video meeting. He noticed the leather case was coming apart. He had super glued it together a few years ago but it was coming apart. He sat in his booth, took a napkin and slowly wedged a tooth pick under each seam of glue and gently piled the removed glue on the napkin. He noticed that the diner was almost full when he came in but he hadn't looked at a single face except the waitress taking his order. Her face was well known, the wife of the manager, a former pro bowler from California. Next to Al's table was four ladies who sat and ate in silence. Each had a faraway look and was not making eye contact with each other. As Al looked around at the other customers, he was shocked.

The diner was filled with thirty four physically/mentally challenged teenagers. Al saw signs of birth defects, signs of oxygen deprivation at birth, signs of disabling early childhood injuries, and a few with Down syndrome. Al went back to pulling glue from his blackberry and thought so this is how we care for these less fortunately people when their families give up. He felt his eyes get wet and felt his cheeks get moist, he thought "this just ain't right for these kids to be abandoned by family." He thought of his own son who had died and when the doctors had requested his permission to end life support because of the damage done to his brain by his very high fever. He refused the doctors request and he thought of how angry and defeated he felt when his son died.

The waitress started bringing the kids burgers and they all started talking at once, the silence ended in a second. Each one knew exactly what their burger must have and must not have. The waitress knew these kids and most of the burgers were exactly as ordered, the ones that weren't as ordered went back for fixing. Some wanted 2 slices of tomato; some only wanted 4 slices of pickle. The all ate with abandon. This trip bowling was their big day out and they were enjoying it as much as the four ladies controlling them would allow. As if on a time table one of the ladies told them to finish eating it was time for bowling. Al did not like her authoritative voice; he concentrated on his blackberry and the glue until as they were all leaving. In the booth behind Al was a teenage boy with downs syndrome who had been watching Al pick glue and cry. Al noticed how neat he was, clothes clean and ironed, every hair on his head neatly trimmed. When he was out of the vision of the four ladies that had turned to go into the bowling alley, he leaned over to Al and asks him "Are you All right?" Al said "yes, thank you. I'm ok". He thought how good it felt just knowing that kid was concerned about him.

As Al was leaving he turned to see bowling balls flying all over the place, some going to other lanes, some going backwards and some just being dropped. He smiled and told himself "I have never felt better". "That one observing kid made everything all alright." Al knew that kid would also help the other kids. He was a real Angel in a funny body.

Al thought of the old Greek proverb "A society is ok as long as old men plant trees whose shade they know they will never sit under" and said to himself "guess I better go and plant a tree so these kids will have a shade to sit under."

Chapter 11

2012 Interstate 10 Road Trip

Al and Gail were married in Las Vegas 38 years ago. They were married on Thanksgiving Day and consider it their anniversary. They decided to drive from Houston to Las Vegas and chance the bad winter weather along the way to celebrating their anniversary. For 38 years they had been going to Vegas to celebrate their anniversary and had never missed a single one. They planned a slow steady drive and to stop overnight as needed. The Escalade was ready to run the 3000 miles to and from Vegas.

They thought that each trip for the past ten years would be their last one. As they drove west along I-10, Al thought of his 40 years of international work and all his friends that his wife and children would never know. Driving just outside Houston they drove past the town of Sealy. Al noticed the old motel that was once the "Second Best Whore House in Texas" was still there but in total demise. He remembered his friends Buddy and Dan had stopped by after a week of deer hunting. When Al looked them up after 30 years he learned they both died of lung cancer, the cancer caused by asbestos and the same kind Al battled for 10 years. He thought to himself "that Dam Company killed them and wounded me". When Al knew them Buddy had just completed 4 years in the Marines and Dan had spent 4 years getting educated and playing in the San Houston State band. Their futures were defined by the company's uncaring use of asbestos.

After they passed the Army truck manufacturing place near Sealy Al recalled his role in helping bring that plant to Texas. During the gulf war the Army had sent out bids for a new generation of the Army trucks 2 and half ton and 5 ton. Al's mother had just passed and his boss wanted him to stay busy, so he assigned al the planning duties for a truck assembly plant in the event the company was successful in getting the bid. The team had 6 members and almost no chance of getting such a large contract. A year later they were awarded the contract and bought the old Cameron valve plant to convert to a truck assembly plant. During that year Al and the other team members traveled to see existing truck factories in the US and Europe, they modeled their configurations after the Austrian Styr company truck. This was the company that had just made new trucks for the Canadian army. Team members exited the company in a few years after being successful in getting the contract. No small event to beat out GM Chrysler, Mercedes and a few other major truck manufactures, but they had a product much better than anyone else. Jim and Mac had built the first truck by hand and rebuilt it so many times; they could build it by hand in just 8 hours. All bolt up assembly but equipped with a new efficient GM engine and an Allison transmission with the ability to inflate or deflate the tires while driving. Paul Ed, Jim, Jim and Mac put their lives on hold while working to get the contract. Sandy was the team leader and he was an old Army Master Sergeant who grew up in Clute Texas and had done his 20 years in Army intelligence. He rarely missed anything and held everyone accountable. A month after getting the contract Sandy had a heart attack and died on a golf course. Jim nr 1 would go back to Michigan to design trucks and Mac would go back to the Rio Grand valley to build busses. Paul Ed's wife died and he would stop work and go back to the South Texas ranch where he grew up. Mac would retire in Galveston and never work again.

The company would lose the contract after the next Democrat was elected, the family members who owned the company got too rich to care and the new truck contract would be given to a company in Wisconsin. Al smiled when he thought of the trucks because he knew the team had set a very high standard for army trucks and the GI's loved them. The entire team had served in the military. He had witnessed the GI's love of that truck first hand in both Gulf wars.

In San Antoine they passed a race track. Al remembered Bill the man he worked with in Indonesia and who is now a construction manger for the largest aluminum company in the world. Bill owned that track until his wife made him sell it because his oldest son was becoming a stock car driver and was doing poor in school, his son went on to win a few NASCA car races. Turned out he was bi polar and driving a car very fast was healthy. Last week bill's youngest son was getting a divorced and Bill called Al from Africa to help him find a lawyer. Al receives weekly emails from Bill.

Al told himself to stop thinking about his friend that his children will never know and almost did so as they drove thru the small town of Mason, Texas. Al remembered a construction manager in Russia who caused Al to become embarrassed. It was a St Patrick day party in Russia and Sam and his new Russian wife was at the party. His mother in law was also there helping with the cooking and because she was younger than Sam, Al assumed that the mother in law was the wife and gave her congratulations on her recent marriage. Only then was he introduced to Sam's 25 year old bride. Al thought, Dam I am really glad my kids won't ever know this man.

Somewhere before leaving Texas Al saw the sign Fort Worth. His eyes teared up and his wife asks if the allergies were bothering him. It wasn't the allergies bothering him; it was his old billionaire friend JB. JB was older than Al's father and a real legendary Texas Billionaire. He owned or held interest in several hundred companies but his love was his memories of being a flying tiger in the Army air force, making his first million by building oil drilling rigs and by owning his own oil company and Swiss Bank. When Al and JB first met it was a business connection gone badly in Zurich Switzerland and JB's son was the reason it went bad. JB called Al in Indonesia to tell him he didn't appreciate Al roughing up his son. When Al visited him in FT Worth, JB came to tears when Al told him how his son screwed up a deal. They would remain friends until JB died at 88 years old. JB's circles of friends were government officials and mostly foreign government officials. Before the first meeting JB had Al completely investigated. When Al learned of the investigation, he had JB investigated completely but JB when he found out he could not make a determination of whom or why someone was investigating him. Al used an associate with no apparent connection or interest in JB. During their first meeting he spoke of Al's father's family and Al spoke of his brothers. The meeting was close to a blood and DNA and because they both so proud of their blood and DNA. After the exam they bonded as only brothers can.

The allergies kept Al's eyes watering until his wife offered him a tissue. Even remembering JB was hard. It was like thinking of his father. Somehow JB knew Al's father but he never told Al how or why he knew his uncles and father. He and JB became friends and business partners. He taught Al more about international banking and politics than he could learn at any college. He told Al that the Swiss banks were going down because of what they had done to the Jews during and after world war two, he told Al that President Clinton would be impeached. More important he told Al more than two years before these events happened. In most of Al's visits to see JB they talked about life and his regrets with his children. He introduced Al to foreign government officials and high level Federal employees. He showed Al a list of the companies that he owned or controlled. He showed Al pictures of his airplane he flew in WWII while he served with the Flying Tigers in China. JB's passing was like losing family.

Driving into New Mexico Al thought of his Army buddy the Pueblo Indian Roger. As they entered Santa Fe Al knew that Roger and his people had ruled this part of New Mexico a thousand years before the arrival of Europeans. Roger had spent his entire Army enlistment time along the Mekong River from Burma to Cambodia. He spoke the languages along the river and at times he would go unarmed to the villages. Once he took Al with him to watch dragon boat races. The villages would make boats from giant teak logs. The boats usually carried more than a hundred people. The villages would challenge another village to a race. It was a matter of pride but also a display of power. They would use wooden paddles coordinated strokes to a drum beat. Seemed to Al the hardest part of the race was floating the hollowed out logs until they were beside each other before starting the race. The village they were in seemed like all innocent villages just having fun until a few weeks later when a US F4 airplane was shot down near the village where they watched the race, the same day, same village two rescue helicopters also got shot down. When Al questioned Roger if he knew the village was all bad guys, Roger just smiled. Roger also took Al to a place full of great looking women, ice cold beer and most of the men visiting the place were North Vietnamese army officers. Only rule while in the place was being a gentleman and no conversations with the other Johns. Roger was a special person, every bit as special as his ancestors. When Roger was in his 60's he would serve as their Chief of the Pueblo's. When they served together in the army he never talked to Al about one day being a Chief; mostly he spoke of his basketball playing at New Mexico State.

The road sign said Eagle Pass and Al thought of his two old friends who found their way to the sacred lawman rank of Texas Ranger. It wasn't easy for either of them. Jerry was a big person but he was so evenly proportioned that he carried his six foot six inch, 280 pound mussel up body with the grace of a gymnast. Unlike most big people Jerry had a bad temper and you were either his friend or his enemy. At best he was complicated. His head football coach at the university said he was the best defensive lineman that he had ever coached. He didn't finish college but went on to play professional football in both Denver and Miami. When he gave up the football for money work he drifted from job to job not really fitting in and his temper and intolerance made sure he changed jobs regularly. After his mother died and Jerry became a Texas Highway patrolman. During his patrolman days they made sure he was always on duty far away from where he grew up. They knew him. And he spent his time in the less populated parts of West Texas. Every time al heard the story of a town having a riot and calling the Governor to send the Texas rangers. When only one ranger showed up the town's people complained to the governor that one ranger was not enough, his response was "well you only reported one riot". Jerry would have been that ranger. When he and Al worked at the state prison there was a prison riot and Jerry and one trustee stopped the riot. The trustee was one of those rare inmates that would never see freedom, never wanted to see freedom. He was the same size as Jerry but his record was one of the most incredible Al had ever read and he was the personal trustee of the warden. No one else could tell him to do anything except the warden. He had been convicted for killing three wives. All three were murdered the same way. He cut off their head off while they were sleeping. Mr. Haynes was the trustee's name and he trained Jerry how to stop a riot but Jerry's bosses at the department of public safety made sure that he was always a very long way from a populated area, even after he became a Texas Ranger he handled the remote parts of West Texas. Jerry was born to be a Texas Ranger and he would never have another job. Jerry was the person who took Al and Jerry's friend Dan to the chicken ranch. It was a fond place for Jerry because it was there that he decided to play football at the University of Texas and it was because of all his visits to the chicken ranch that he flunked out of school. Not even Jerry could understand Haynes killing three wives and somehow remaining the sanest person anyone had ever known. It was always obvious that even Haynes didn't understand Haynes. Lots of memories as Al drove thru West Texas. Al was sure Dan had also become a Texas Ranger because of Jerry. Al wondered if their paths would cross again. He hoped it would but it had been a long time.

CHAPTER 12

2014 JIMMY LEE

Winter came with vengeance. The cold arctic winds reached Texas and cut thru the skies as if the might gulf of Mexico winds were reduced to a mere breeze. The sycamore tree leaves that had provided summer shade were now being blown around the ground looking for a place to rot. The horses and cows quickly started growing winter hair and the green grasses of summer were a light brown. Another season of Al's life was starting and he wondered if he had the resistance and will power to live thru another season. It seemed as if his every trip to the doctor would resemble reading a horoscope of the blood. Good cholesterol too low, bad cholesterol too high, PSA spiking and common allergies triggering respirator infections. The dog Whoopi was missing and Al feared the worst. He concluded that because of her fighting skills and people friendly spirit that she had been stolen to be used to train Pit Bulldogs to fight or maybe it was the alligator she had been stalking for months that had finally gotten her. Al filled two clips of hollow point bullets for his 45 caliber 1911 model and waited for news from the Pit Bulldog people or a glimpse of the alligator but no news came except from his cousin Jimmy Lee. Jimmy Lee was dying. He had liver cancer, kidney cancer and kidney failure. He would be taking dialysis as long as he lived but no one gave him much of a chance for anything except a quick and painless death. Al planned a trip to see him and talk to him and to say goodbye.

Jimmy Lee and Al had been close even though life had carried them in many different directions but when their paths crossed there was always fond discussion of their childhoods spent growing up in the Piney woods of east Texas. Al had memories of them running barefooted thru the woods hunting down snakes, digging in the old Indian graveyards and playing rodeo with the wild cows. It seemed that all the fun things they did as children were always done under a threat of a beating by their parents. Safety first was not an option for boys growing up in the woods. The promised beatings from their parents never materialized but there were more than a few trips to the nearest emergency room for repairs to their young bodies. Jimmy Lee had a body like his father. Tall, heavy, muscled up and a natural strength that made fighting him always a poor choice. He would be nicknamed Bull and it fit but underneath the big frame was a docile, caring and understanding person that made people smile. His father Oscar had served in WWII with the Army in Europe. He served under General "blood and guts" Patton and came home with lots of war medals and a medal plate in his head. In Germany they have a mock battle field for practicing war, its name Graffenware. The Germans have probably used Graffenware for practicing for every one of their wars. The battlefield has been used since the Germans first started throwing sticks and rocks at each other and General Patton is the only non German general in their Graffenware war museum. By all accounts Patton was a general who was born to direct fighting men and Oscar served with him until late in the war. In the battle of the budge where he would be wounded and half of his scull replaced with a steel plate to keep his brains in. When Oscar came home as a war hero and disabled veteran all was well. He married Jimmy Lee's mother and they produced twelve children. His wife Doris died giving birth to the last child. Jimmy Lee was the second born and the closest to a clone of his father with the demur and manners of his Grand Mother.

Oscar's main problem was no one would give a job to a disabled vet and for years the family watched as Oscar struggled to support his wife and children by farming. Finally it was decided that he must get a job. For months Al's mother and her niece Cora would drive Oscar to places of employment. After months of looking Oscar finally got a job in a foundry. He finally had a way to support his family. He would keep that job all his life. Their family had grown to twelve children.

Jimmy Lee's growing up was normal but was forever changed when his brother Billy Mac, who was one year older, got drafted by the Army and sent to Viet Nam. His older brother was killed during his first month in country. Jimmy Lee's life would never be the same. The gentile giant was awakened and only after he started working in the oil fields on a drilling rig did he find semblance of a normal, happy life. Al and Al's brother Joe would also be forced to take a detour on the way to happiness because when Billy Mac was killed they both learned that war is very personal. Joe had been in the Army since his 17th birthday, he had done his time as a paratrooper, and then started flying helicopters; he had already completed two tours in Viet Nam and his only comment had been to say "killing people is too dam easy." Al had been in the Army for 3 years and ready to get out and come home. He had been in Special Operations in Germany, living in Bavaria watching the Russians invade Czechoslovak, he didn't wear a uniform every day and the army was just a job. They were both professional soldiers and knew that there was nothing personal about war but all that changed when Billy Mac got killed. They both lied to the Army and their wives so they could go to Viet Nam at the same time and revenge Billy Mac's death. 1968 had been a life changing year.

Driving alone to the funeral Al thought of the roads he traveled. Highway 59 ran from the Mexican border to Houston then it turned north to Arkansas. At the town of Corrigan highway 59 intersects with highway 287. Highway 287 starts at Port Author and rambles up to Canada. Janis Joplin was from Port Author and her music still plants a beat and some thoughts into the minds of listeners. Even today there was a mystery about how and why she died so young. She was a face and a sound of the counter culture movement that swept America in the 60's and forty years later some people still thought about her being killed by the government. Her candle burned short, bright and too fast. Al thought her music sounded like Memphis blues adapted to California hard rock but he still listened to and liked her music.

The turn west on to highway 287 from highway 59 was always an adventure of dodging log trucks that were coming out of the forest hauling logs to and lumber from the nearby saw mills. Most of the towns in east Texas were former sawmill towns or railroad towns. A few miles out of Corrigan there are markers for a town that no longer exist. Sumter was once the county seat of Trinity County but after the civil war it was burned to the ground and all that remains today are a cemetery and the historical marker. As the crow flies Sumter is 8 miles from where Al, Jimmy Lee and their brothers grew up. Not such an interesting place except that small town produced one of the old west's meanest/smartest outlaws. John Wesley Hardin was raised there and killed his first two men there. While serving time in Texas prison he earned his Law degree and worked as a lawyer before he was killed by a client. When the federal government built highway 287 it had some military purpose. The authorities wanted a road from a port along the Gulf of Mexico to go across Indian country all the way to Canada. As a young man John Wesley was traveling on the road which travel was forbidden to the locals. Many of the locals had not redeclared their oath of allegiance to the United States of America and the Union carpetbaggers who were ruling the county and state governments? An argument started with the road builders and the son of a Methodist preacher won the argument by killing his first 2 men. Hind sight said they should have let him use the road. Strange as it seems some of Harding's relatives still live in these woods and Al, his brothers and Jimmy Lee went to school with them. Al didn't recall any of Harding's relatives ever speaking about their famous relative but he knew they would be attending Jimmy Lee's funeral.

Al's wife usually picked out his clothes to wear to church and funerals but this day she did not. Al had no idea what men's ware was fashionable but he tried his best to choose the right suite, shirt and tie. He knew it would not be what his wife would choose but he really didn't care. He only considered dress because at the last funeral most of the men in his family were wearing thousand dollar Italian suites and real silk ties. He wondered how a bunch of hillbilly relatives who lived in the same houses they were born in even knew how to get a tailor made Italian silk suite. He thought about it and decided that his thousand dollar custom made Lucchese boots would be his fashion statement that they would all notice his boots and maybe they would forget about his ten year old Hong Kong tailored suit and his mismatched shirt and tie. He also knew that the funeral would be part funeral and part homecoming. The real funeral would be at the grave and when the casket was lowered and the first shovel of dirt was thrown in. In the past all family funerals were preceded by a 3 day wake with the deceased laying in a coffin in the living room of their home but new generations and new traditions. Al remembered at his fathers wake when he and his brothers talked to their father and making promises to remember what he had taught them. He remembered that his father didn't wear any ring; Al took off his Masonic ring and placed on his father's finger for burial. He remembered that one year his father had sold his own Masonic ring to buy Al and his brothers Christmas presents. Al never wore another ring after his father's wake. Time had passed too quickly there were no more family wakes.

The week before the funeral Al's visit to the hospital to visit and talk to Jimmy Lee it was time well spent. He was hooked up to a dialysis machine but recognized Al when he walked in the room. His wife of many years introduced herself and told Al she had heard of him and was pleased to meet him. Al stood by Jimmy Lee and they talked as if they were kids. They made each other laugh and the young doctor who was quietly viewing the results of the dialysis turned to listen to their stories. No quarter spared, none ask. After questioning about whether dialysis could remove all the whiskey he had drank in his life Al noticed the wife smiling. He knew Jimmy Lee didn't drink. He asks her how she ever got hooked up with Jimmy Lee. When she answered that she had been asking herself the same question. As she politically explained how she met Bull, he was smiling as if to say yes it was love at first sight, you are not telling the entire story and yes you were putty in my hands. When she said they met while Bull was working in Oregon, Al commented that he had two real good friends from Oregon and he had taken a vacation there but the next time he went there he was going to kick his friends' butts. She ask why and he said that without any question Oregon is the most beautiful state in America and all the years he had known his friends they had to listen to Al tell about Texas but not once did they ever tell about the beauty of Oregon. Yes they spoke of resentment to people from California changing the every day life in Oregon. Al promised to kick his friend's butts because they never spoke of Oregon; they both had replied "Well we are not Texans". She fully understood and laughed at the humor. When Al said goodbye and walked out of the room she followed him and said "you know he is not leaving the hospital. Al said "yes I know, call me if you need any help." Five days later he was driving down hwy 287 to the funeral. Thinking about how well this lady from Oregon fits into this family. That day in the hospital he could see their love and strengths. Few people are so lucky to have known unquestionable love and strength thru death. That lady is a real special Oregon rose.

The funeral home chapel was almost empty when Al arrived because he was an hour early. He sat in his truck and watched people go inside. He really hated to go inside. His brother had told him the ceremony would be administered by a Church of Christ preacher and he didn't know what to expect but thought it would something about get your sorry ass right with God before it's too late. Four of Grandpa's brothers had been preachers and Al had heard those sermons most of his life. Al had made his peace with God 4 or 5 years after Viet Nam and the only time he had questioned God was when his younger brother Fred had died. He had prayed for his survival for more than a year but his prayers weren't answered. The defeat had preceded a five year work assignment in Russia and in some strange way the Russians who were prohibited worship of any kind had renewed Al's reconciliation with God. He was at peace with God and when he really thought he would die with cancer because the doctors told him he would, he thought about how great it would be to again see his brother, son, parents, grandparents, friends. Now Jimmy Lee would be seeing those same people. He thought it strange that he kind of admired Jimmy Lee.

The second he saw Jimmy Lee's family tears started to flow. He spoke with all of them as they all wiped uncontrollable tears away. The people at the funeral were mostly family and relatives but there were many of his coworkers. Men that he had spent many days and nights with him drilling oil wells and they probably knew him better than his own family. Al quickly bonded with the drillers and when Jimmy Lee's brother asked Al to set up front with the family, he chose to set with the drillers because he knew his tears would be noted by the family as a kind of weakness because the family believes you should cry and pray in private. But setting with the drillers he would be ok with his tears and Al could already see tears in their eyes.

Al didn't worry any more about fashion because Jimmy Lee made his own fashion statement by requesting to be buried in his work clothes. The blue and white stripped overalls were spotless and his wife had starched and ironed them until they looked like new army kakis'. He could see the love in the way the old work clothes were washed. His favorite designer hard hat was placed on his chest. All the overseas workers had a hat like that. Al had one at home, so he knew exactly how much it meant to Jimmy Lee. You don't buy those hats they are gifts from your friends, friends that your family will never meet. There was no spare room in the coffin because Jimmy Lee filled it up.

The preacher had been Jimmy Lee's best friend and before the funeral started Al had noticed him in the refreshment area of the chapel in deep prayer. He started the sermon by saying that when Jimmy Lee's wife had ask him if he would preach the funeral she should have ask if he could preach the funeral of his life time best friend. Then he talked about them growing up together and going off to college together. He said when they played basketball how everyone laughed at the way Jimmy Lee ran up and down the court but the other team quickly learned which spot on the court belonged to Jimmy Lee and people were always surprised because he averaged scoring 35 points a game from his spot. He knew him well and Al was a little surprised to learn Jimmy Lee had graduated from college and how he made both of the Deans lists. The first Deans list he made was the academic probation list; the last list was just the Deans list. The preacher said that no one did more for the church and its people than Jimmy Lee. His approach to church was just like his approach to basketball and drilling. Al suspected Jimmy Lee originally wanted to be a teacher and basketball coach but the oil patch had been a natural job for him. Al knew this because over the years he had talked to him at work and about work. Drilling is a job where you have to trust others with your life and no one understood that better than the man they all called Bull.

After the funeral Al spoke with Jimmy Lee's brother who was also a driller. He told him that 10 years ago their uncle Jesse had told him to look in to their father's death. He thought there was some foul play when Oscar died. Al said he didn't follow their uncle's request because he trusted that if it needed to be looked into Jimmy Lee would have done it and he was a little upset that his uncle had not followed family protocol. Now was the time for them to follow their uncle's request. Al's next stop after the funeral was at his retired vice cop cousin's house. Wayne was recently retired so happy to have some real cop work to do and Al knew that by the time of his next visit they would have a trail to follow. Al would follow the trail his way, face to face with the bad guys after first hand shadowing them, observing their habits and getting to know everything about them. Al's Cousin Wayne would work the bad guy's history files and records. Al knew that it would all come together and if the bad guys had said anything to anybody Wayne would find out because like most old cops his real friends were mostly former bad guys. Al thought the bad guys who may have killed Oscar were probably already in prison because he thought they were a part of the white extremist group and meth dealers that like to live deep in the woods. The Feds had rounded up most of them after the national news that some of them pulled a black man behind a truck until his head fell off. Al thought to himself I don't owe this to Jimmy Lee, I owe this to my Uncle Jesse and dam if I don't wish I had started this earlier when I was younger and healthy. He thought "Oh well I suppose there is never a wrong time to do the right thing ... but this thing will come together real hard and fast so you better get ready."

Then he thought about his family's grandkids he had seen at the funeral and how much they looked and acted like his own grand children. Strong, tough and sensitive would describe them well. If someone had killed their grandpa they deserved both the truth and some justice and he also deserved an answer about what happened to his dog Whoopi.

CHAPTER 13

2015 THE STEW MAN

Paul Ed had not paid a visit in more than two years. Paul Ed's wife had passed away and he was spending time alone on his South Texas ranch. He was spending weeks alone in the wilds. His horse was his only transport and at night he slept on the ground with only a lariat rope formed in a circle around him to keep snakes away. He was well schooled by the Army in living off the land. His 22 cal pistol provided his food. Al had heard this from friends about Paul Ed and wondered what was in his brain but he knew all was well and Paul Ed was just making peace with himself after the death of his wife. He was reliving his youth. Time is the best healer of wounded hearts.

When Paul Ed showed up at Al's farm in the spring he looked healthier that Al ever remembered even though his eyes told the story. He had lost at least 50 pounds, his skin was much tanned and he had that crazy look that Al had seen in three wars. He was ready for something but Al didn't have a clue what he was ready for. In all the years they had known each other Al never fully understood what went on in Paul Ed's Jew brain, but somehow it didn't really matter.

Al told him that their friend Sam the preacher had died and his "medal of honor winning combat medic son" had retired from the city of Houston, Raffel had been fired by the ranch owner he was working for and was now working at a Jack in the Box in the next town. He hadn't seen him in a year or so but saw his girlfriend every now and then and she said he was ok. All is well. Paul said he knew about Sam because he had just come from a visit with the son of Sam. Apparently Sam left him enough developer money to retire in style. Sam had a few thousand acres of land in the Brazos river bottom that no one ever wanted except some land developer from Houston. Sam was not only a preacher he was a good business man and remarkably half of the national basketball league players lived in homes built by Houston land developers on land once owned by Sam. The land was south of the old sugar mill and the town named Sugarland and was surrounded by a host of Texas prison farms. After America's civil war most of the land changed titles from the plantation owners to the state of Texas because the taxes could not be paid. Al knew he paid for all the land by buying and selling scrap medal. Al missed Sam's sermons and Sam had a way of showing up in Al's life just when he needed him and his sermons. That look in Paul Ed's eyes told Al that he really needed one of Sam's sermons.

Paul Ed's arrival was like a hurricane. After the death of his wife he had been living off the land on his family's ranch in South Texas. His half brother Juan was missing and he suspected that he was a victim of the Drug Cartels. Juan had retired as a Major in the Army and after retirement he traveled the Southwest with his girlfriend on a motor cycle. As Paul Ed spoke with his blue eyes shinning, Al could see the rage and he knew that Paul Ed had a plan to find his brother. More than 100,000 people have died along the Mexico/ Texas border and no one spoke about it, the press and media didn't report it and most folks seemed to think that the people got killed because they were involved with the multi billion dollar drug and money criminals. So many drug cartels that one needed a flow chart just to identify their names, apparently it didn't matter to Paul Ed that the bad guys numbered in the hundreds of thousands and with connections ranging from china to Europe. Seemed that the only time anything was reported to the public about the drug war body count was when a politician or a policeman was involved or killed. The Mexican and American people just didn't care.

Paul Ed's plan was to go to the border and find his brother. Al thought "I hope we have enough bullets for this adventure but he didn't worry because he knew there would be few bullets fired because this was much too personal and Paul Ed wanted to see there eyes as the people who brought harm to his brother died. Al told him he would meet him in Eagle Pass in two days, and then he thought I better make sure that I say anything to the family that needs saying and tell a friend or two where to look for him if he didn't come back.

Al had no idea where this trip would end so he packed his Chevy Avalanche for a month stay. He told his wife he had some family business in east Texas but his Avalanche headed West on I10. He thought of what the wife said when he bought the Avalanche in 2002. "Why so much plastic on the sides and why didn't you buy a truck?" None the less the Avalanche had almost 200,000 miles driven and everything still worked. She would always say "this is the most comfortable vehicle we have ever owned." On this day the side saddles were loaded with ammo and the back was full of guns. A sawed off 16ga loaded with buckshot was lying in the back seat under a heavy shirt. No need to worry because it won't change what already is. Just be prepared, think positive, and think out of the box. Al thought to himself "100,000 people have already died in this drug war and now I am going looking for it, I am really rally too dam old for this crap. My golden years seem to have way too much lead surrounding me."

The drive to Eagle Pass was a sight to behold. The entire surround area was full of drilling rigs and oil field workers. He met Paul Ed across the border in Eagle Pass. He was already with his soldier friends and had already told them the story of his missing brother. They agreed to help but warned Paul Ed to not take unnecessary chances. They all knew Juan and had served in training with them. Across the border from El Paso was a killing field and it wasn't safe for anyone to be there at night or day. Seems the west coast drug cartels from Sinaloa and Tijuana had been trying to take over the drug routes that ran thru El Paso. Paul Ed told them that he just wanted to find his brother. They had already provided weapons and ammo for the trip, mostly some C4 explosives and a few rocket launchers and a couple of 50 calibers and for some reason they gave Paul Ed a new knife. It was a small one with only a 3 inch blade. As they spoke Paul Ed was listening and sharpening his new toy with a rock he had picked up from the ground. Paul Ed had taught Al how to sharpen a knife and he did so without looking at the blade. He listened to the sound the steel and rock were making. When he finished you could shave with any knife that he sharpened.

They drove into the night and stopped about thirty miles East of El Paso. They unloaded the four wheelers and strapped on a tank of gasoline and drove along the Mexican border. With in five miles from the border they smelled the stench of the dead. They approached the smell and did some investigating of the large concrete tanks. They decided that the tanks had been tanks used to make leather for the boot factories in El Paso but the lack of security around the place or the sight of people made the awful smell in the air made it surreal. After a few minutes an old Mexican man came out and asked what they wanted and if he could do for them. Paul Ed asked what was the horrible smell that seemed to acidic and was causing burns to the eyes and nose. The old man told them he would show them if they really wanted to know. It was daylight when the old man climbed up the ladder and opened the top of one of the tanks. I was full of dissolving human flesh. The old man said that there were too many people being killed and someone had to take care of the bodies. The tanks contained Caustic acid and he was paid to dispose of them by who ever brought them to him. Paul Ed told the old man that we were looking for his brother. He described his brother and then Paul Ed took out his Army dog tags and told the old man that his brother would have been wearing tags like these. The old man moved his head towards the wooden house that he came from and requested that they join him. Inside the house he opened a wooden trunk and told Paul Ed to look thru the items he had removed from the pit after the bodies were dissolved. Paul Ed looked thru the rings, teeth fillings, bracelets until he found his brothers dog tags. He thanked the old man, took his brothers dog tags and told Al that it was time for him to go home he would handle the rest of dealing with his brother's death and he needed some time alone.

Al was setting on the four wheeler and getting ready to go home when a black truck drove up the canyon blowing his horn and flashing his lights. He put the sawed off shotgun down the leg of his pants and walked over to stand along side Paul Ed. When the truck stopped, the driver shouted "where is the stew man, I have some business for him" The old man was walking over to meet the horn blowing customer when Paul Ed struck. In a split second he stabbed the horn blower in the heart with this three inch knife, then as he slumped down to his knees Paul Ed cut his jugular vein and when his head fell down and his blood pumped out on the ground Paul Ed drove the knife blade thru the top of his neck completely cutting thru his spine. Any of the three wounds were fatal but he knew the rage Paul Ed was feeling and didn't want to see a moving dead man

The stew man walked up to the dying man completely unfazed and asks Paul Ed what the man had wanted. He opened the back of the truck and showed the old man the bodies to be disposed of. Paul Ed opened his wallet pulled out a hundred dollar bill and told the old man that the man forgot to include himself. He then told him I will be sending you some more business, just keep a count and I will pay you later. A one man killing machine was just unleashed. Paul Ed told Al that he would come to see him when he had evened the score. Al told him that their old friend from Laos who was now a chief of the Pueblos and told him to not be afraid to look him up if he needed a place to hide out. Paul Ed smiled and said don't worry, it will go one way or the other and I really don't care but I am not going to hide out until I find out who is running this drug war.

Al told Paul Ed if he needed him that he knew where to find him then he drove home alone, he didn't remember seeing or hearing anything for the entire 800 mile drive. When he pulled into his front gate he spoke out loud "where to hell is that dam dog?"

CHAPTER 14

2014 CHICKEN LEGS

Sometimes we get to see things that bring back so many good memories of what we Americans are about. I had just watched the last game of the baseball World Series and before the play offs started my good friend (who is a consultant to the Los Angeles Dodgers and the source of many of my free baseball tickets), were talking baseball. I don't get to see many baseball games because our new team owner has all but blacked out the local market and other owners are in favor of pay for view only, forgetting that greed is a threat to the fan base. Of course my friend bleeds Dodger blue and I am a Houston Astros fan. Astros have been in a rebuild after changing owners and leagues. In my childhood the Houston team was a minor league team of the St Louis Cardinals. I choose Astros first and Cardinals second but in our conversation I mentioned that the best team I had seen playing this year was the Kansas City Royals. The Royals were playing good ball and didn't appear to have any weakness but I mentioned that in the other league I liked the San Francisco Giants. Of course the Giants are the dark and dreary enemy of my friends beloved Dodgers. He felt sure the Dodgers were a run away favorite because they had the best pitcher and hitter in baseball. I reminded him that the best hitter in baseball was the new Astros second baseman who stands about five feet and four inches tall. He questioned me why I liked the Giants and I told him that their right fielder was both me and my wife's favorite player. He had started out as an Astros player and had been traded to the Giants shortly after the new owner arrived. We had watched him play since he was a rookie and no one had more enthusiasm for the game. He played the game the way everyone should play, as a young boy having a great time. I reminded him of our last trip to the ball park and my friend and me standing in center field and holding up both arms for him to hit a homer in our direction. He saw us but didn't hit a homer in that at bat but his very next at bat he hit a home run to the same spot where we had been standing in. My friend didn't agree with my choice of the Giants so I told him the Giants first baseman was from my home town in East Texas and it was his high school baseball field was where I got my first hit in high school baseball, I was a fourteen year old freshman and most of the high school players were 17 or 18 years old. That first hit kind of changed the game for me because I learned that in the batters box no one can help you and when the ball is hit to you no one can help you catch it and when you throw the ball no one can make it go fast and straight to the target except you. In spite of these requirements to be a base ball player; Baseball is a true team sport where you success or failure depends not only on yourself or your best players but on the ability of all the other players. I became a fan of other players. I also mentioned that I liked their third baseman. I had watched him since he was a rookie and thought he may well eat his way out of the big leagues. I suppose he had some kind of eating disorder but I had thought that his weight and eating habits may restrict his abilities but considering where he came from eating was probably his only security. Fat or not he hustled every at bat, every fielding chance and every time on base, he seemed to have a special zone that got more special in big games and who could not like their manager. He also was an ex Astros catcher and was a no non sense guy who knew his players and their limits. I thought that would be the difference when the game was on the line. My friend and I agreed to disagree.

Then I thought of my first and last visit to San Francisco. My first visit was while I was in the Army and on my way to Vietnam. Because my group was special operations we were not sent to directly to the Army replacement in Oakland we were sent up to a field station near Petaluma. Some delays in our travel and the base commander decided to assign my unit to grunt duties which included polishing his office brass every night. He seemed to have a great affection for all the brass door knobs and brass plates in his office. After a week of my unit cleaning his crap we revolted and refused to perform the duties. A few days later our own General decided to move us to Oakland but with restrictions to base. All the Army guys coming from Vietnam came through that replacement center to be processed out of the Army. I remember one night one of my unit's members told me that he thought that all the returning vets were crazy and I told him to remember that these were the ones who came home. The others came home in body bags. We learned this at that replacement center and we also learned that being restricted to base did not mean we couldn't walk out the gate, hire a taxi and go in to San Francisco. Of course we all headed to the Height Ashbury area to visit with the war protestors and hippies. Somehow we all fit in together and my group read the anti war protestors and their supporting people as just being plain afraid. They read us as being just plain crazy. We didn't have any trouble with fitting into the crowd of lost souls. San Francisco was also the place where Army guys went to before deciding to go to Canada as deserters. The hippie chicks were a different matter and most of them were just into weed. Weed was unknown to us because we had been serving in the Army in Europe for the past 3 years. One soldier in another unit spent some time in the Decau army prison because he would not shave his mustache. Heaven only knows what they would have done to us for using dope of any kind. This was the same Decau prison that had witnessed the holocaust in World War 2. A place I visited and could feel its evil presence. It was good observation and lessons well learned because some of us would get a PHD in weed before the Army was through with us. We all enjoyed San Francisco and our last view of America was the Golden Gate Bridge. On board the airplane to Viet Nam we all silently prayed that we would return to see that bridge.

My last trip to San Francisco was after my battle with lung cancer. The radiation and chemo had almost killed me. My wife and I decided to take a month long driving vacation to celebrate my survival. There would be more chemo later but we needed to go somewhere new and get a fresh view point on life. We drove to Denver then on to Portland Oregon. We stayed in some town in northern Nevada during a bikers rally and saw lots of miles of little towns and Portland was a great three day stop. We decided to drive the Pacific coast road from Portland to San Francisco and the drive thru the redwood forest and Napa valley kind of spoke to our soul. The bridges of Oregon was educational and after not eating well on the trip we decided to stop somewhere in grape country. The motel was old and cheap but the old restaurant nearby was not cheap. Because it was the only one in the area we just walked in and sat down. We tried to read a slightly wore out menu. The waitress came over and told us she would order for us. I probably wanted a red steak and the wife wanted some fish. I felt insulted but the waitress won and walked away. She came back later with the best food imaginable. Weeks later I would look up the restaurant on the internet to discover it was one of the top five in America. We definitely got our moneys worth and the next day we dove across the Golden Gate Bridge and into San Francisco. The beauty and memories were overpowering. We headed straight to Fisherman's Warf for mid afternoon snack.

After the snack we drove around the city. Much had changed since 1968, no hippies, no war protestors, not so many downtown strip clubs and mostly just people going about their daily lives. Yet there was something different. On closer observation it seemed that every business, every restaurant every place I looked I saw gay people. Not people posing as gay, just gay people being normal. I thought that this must be a refuge of sorts where gay people can live with out any notice or special treatment. The sight was something as beautiful as the flowers the hippie girls use to wear in their hair and on their clothes. I doubt there any other place in the world where gays can live as normal. There was absolutely nothing that was not normal with what I was seeing. I felt a tear run down my cheek and I thought of what most of these people must have suffered before they found their way to San Francisco.

We left town to see cannery row and the place where John Steinbeck my favorite author wrote his books. I thought about how much time he must have spent on the streets of San Francisco.

The World Series had proven to be a classic. I told my Dodger friend that the next time I pick a winner to go to Vegas and make a bet for me. I watched every game and wasn't surprised with the hard fought Giants win. The Royals lived up to their name but in the end the Giants right fielder, third baseman and first baseman refused to lose. A 25 year old Giant pitcher from North Carolina made sure the Giants won by giving up only one run in 3 different games. The Giants didn't have the best pitcher in baseball or the best hitters, neither did the Royals but the series was like watching children play, giving it their all on every play. There were no losers in this World Series. One team scored one more run.

On the day before the last game the national news paper ran a headline that Hunter Pence had turned the World Series into his play pen. He seemed to be having too much fun. I read the headline to the wife and she said "Chicken Legs" is having a good time. She gave him that nickname during his Astros's rookie season.

CHAPTER 15

2002 CHIMAYO

2002 Bugs

I felt a little tired, Siberia was gray and cold
We went to see the Vegas lights but still I felt tired and old
When I came home the doctor told me why
Seems some bug had made a nest in my lung, the ambulance ride gave no peace of mind
I went to the city of Angels in Houston, a cure to find

The next two days I looked inside and wondered why
This wasp of a virus had chose to make me die
I thought of my family, friends and loves
I didn't believe it was all as bad as it sounded but I couldn't look anyone in the eye
To again see my Mother, Father and son was why

Then came the cart and they strapped me down so tight
I had no will to resist; I had no reason to fight
I felt a needle or two go in my arm, no pain no fright
If this life was over, I knew I always tried to do it right

Two days later I woke up and felt such horrible pain

The morphine pump had failed, a doctor was replacing it, the pain
was hell
Every touch I felt a broken bone moving until the new pump
kicked in
A nurse ask if I was ok and I said "Please, not the dam pump
salesmen again"

The next face I saw was the infectious smile of my wife
The same special smile I had seen most of my life
She told me I was crying in my sleep, she had told me that it's ok
We all have to pass this world, each in our own way
But I had told her that I had things to do and didn't want to die
I had to build her a chicken house but she didn't understand why
Because we had no chickens

Three weeks later I was back in Siberia; it was grey and cold as before
But then I saw the sun lighting up a sky of snow outside my door
Like a million diamonds falling gently down to earth making a floor
A beauty like this I had never seen and I ask my Russian friend why:
In Texas old folks say if it rains when the sun is shinning. The Devil
is beating his wife, what do Russians say when it snows and the sun
shines?
He looked at me slowly, confused and said "it would be a hell of a
lot colder without the sunshine"

Ok you slime bastard wasp, Looks like I won this round, now
bug off. It was only round one of the fight.

The Cancer had been operated on and the surgery was successful
but two years later it returned. The chemo and radiation had lasted
another six years and trips to the doctor had become a ritual of
new types of radiation and new chemo drugs. After eight years the
medical treatment of the cancer fighting doctors and machines
had advanced by magnitudes. The detection of cancer had gone
from finding tumors to finding cancer cells. Some of the earlier

experimental chemo drugs had become standard practice, radiation had become a precision targeting of cells and many lives were being extended by the good oncologist but the not so good doctors were killing or crippling people. If patients were not treated and monitored closely many would lose their kidneys and die. So many patients suffered burned out kidneys during treatment that clinics to perform dialysis could now be found in shopping centers.

The rounds of chemo and radiation were done in clinics and I began to make other cancer patient friends. We were all with different cancers and in different stages. I was a category three. The time spent in waiting rooms was informative as the patients exchanged their experiences. Seems lung cancer may not show up until brain cancer is well underway and seizures come with brain cancer. There were many funny stories by these patients. Life goes on and most of the patients continued their employment lives. I noticed that most of the serious patients always came with a brother or sister. My own brother came with me every trip to the doctor and I didn't know why. We had competed with each other all our lives and we were each others worst critics but each visit he would go with me and I always insisted that I did the driving. It must have been funny for him riding home with the driver loaded with chemo of all kinds. I did notice that at times his knuckles would turn white as he was holding on for his life. The spouses and children seemed more stressed and even a visit to the doctor or clinic seemed to drain their spirits. The rounds of chemo and radiation would last eight years before my doctor declared a very uncertain victory. It seems that no one knows why they get cancer and doctors don't know why some patients live and some die. There was lots of uncertainty that comes from living with cancer

During the seventh year I ask my doctor if I could go back to work. He looked at me with a puzzled look and told me that most patients do go back to work and it seems to help them. He must have thought "Are you kidding me?"

I called a working friend from my days in Russia. He told me about the job in Denver and he wanted me to join him and the project that was trying to produce oil and gas from just south of Yellowstone Park. He thought that the Denver air would be good for my lungs and he needed me at work. I started making plans to go work in Denver with much support from anyone but I had enough of taking chemo then spending weeks on the living room sofa. Most of the hair had grown back but I started shaving my head on a daily basis in support of the new friends that I had made in the clinics.

I wanted to make the trip to Denver a memory. The wife and I would drive there, I would live in a hotel, she would fly home and we would take one day at a time. I started looking at maps and decided that a stop over in Santa Fe New Mexico would be in order. It was only 4 or 5 hundred miles longer than the direct route. Surely there must be something to see in Santa Fe if nothing more that the Santa Fe Trail that pioneers took on their way from mid America to California. Then one day in my goggles of interesting places I found out that a small town just North of Santa Fe is the third most visited place in New Mexico. Its name was Chimayo. The information found on Chimayo was almost a mystery. All information about Chimayo was very cautious and politically correct and almost all of it started with stories told of a certain Spanish priest that had been with the soldiers keeping journals of their efforts to Christian Indians.

During the 1500's and 1600's the Spanish had come to Mexico to spread their version of the Christian religion but when they discovered that Mexico had tons and tons of gold and silver that they could easily steal and send back to Spain they caught gold fever. The soldiers would search for the source of the tons and tons of gold. Strict orders from the Queen of Spain clearly stated that the soldier's mission was religion but gold fever was rampant among the Spaniards. Mexico is one of the most diverse countries in the world with more than 200 written and spoken languages but word of the conquering Spaniards traveled faster that their Armies. The

Indians had a news grapevine that was much faster than the soldiers could march. They knew the Spaniards were just looking for gold; so the Indians made up a story that told them to keep going North because further North was a place with so much gold that there were seven cities made of nothing but gold. This story kept them going until they reached Santa Fe and then all hell broke loose. The soldiers knew they had been lied to because they couldn't go any further and the Pueblo Indians were unlike any other Indians they had encountered. The Spaniards started killing Pueblos and the Pueblos started killing Spaniards. During this killing period the young priest who been with the soldiers and keep a journal of the Native Americans they had encountered on the journey. He was just North of Santa Fe when he observed sick Indians going towards a small hole in the earth. There they would take out sand and rub it on their bodies for healing. He also noted that they were being healed. It would be years later before someone in the church read his chronicles and came to investigate. The healing power of the sand proved to be real because after his first visit to Chimayo the PET scans never found another cancer cell in his body. Three hundred years later it is still one of Americas best kept secrets.

CHAPTER 16

1954 EL TORO

Three boys growing up near a National forest earns them a lot of freedom. Joe, Alan, and Fred were 11, 9 and 7 years old and were always playing in the forest when schooling didn't raise its ugly head. Joe was less than five foot tall, Al was just over four feet tall and Fred was three and a half feet tall. The boys all had dark tans from the summer sun. They played war, big game hunter, and wild life tracker. A foot print of a big cat sent chills thru them and their fear was over come by knowing they had secretly borrowed their mother's kitchen knife for their defense. The farms surrounding the National forest were always a 40 acre track of farm land. The farms were all perfect rectangles. The farming of the land was almost finished and most land owners had full time jobs in the local factories and raised cattle as a cash crop. The farms all belonged to either family or in-laws families. Almost everyone still living on the land were family cousins but during the depression and in world war two most of the people had moved away to Houston to find work and would never return to their family farms. Pine trees would eventually take over the fields and change the entire landscape of a farming culture into a timber culture. Their family farm had been passed down to their father after grandpa and grandma had passed away. The once thriving farms were now just pastures filled with cows and horses and the farms were now the playground for three young boys.

The Texas summers can be brutally hot and the forest seemed to fill up with bugs; of all the bad bugs the absolute worst were the small ticks that everyone called seed ticks. They would get on you by the hundreds if your body came in contact with a tree branch or a bush where they lived. They become almost invisible until they had borrowed in to your skin and become festered. The large ticks were easy to spot and remove, if they had locked their blood sucking head into your skin they could be easily removed by holding a burning cigarette near them and watch as the ticks withdrew their heads and tried to make a retreat. Smashing a large tick was easy work but seed ticks were not easy to spot or remove, usually they weren't noticed until a skin sore was found with a small brown dot in the center. Then they were doctored by swabbing with alcohol and covered with iodine. Every day of the boys lives were spent checking for ticks and removing them. The best way to remove them and to cool down was to go swimming. Two farms over the boys Uncle had the perfect swimming hole but they were prohibited from swimming in the Uncles stock pond. The prohibition was tested daily because in the summer months they swam in the pond almost daily. Permission to go fishing was easily obtained but swimming was prohibited and punishable by a whopping of the legs with a switch. The boys were allowed to go and pick out the switch to be used in their punishment. Fishing was always a cover story for swimming. After swimming they would stop on the way home to carefully rub enough dirt on their hands and face to eliminate their mothers doubt about their swimming. The alternative to going swimming was having their mother bath them in the wash tub with water heated in the giant iron pot and they were washed with a home made Lye soap. Swimming was more civilized and certainly it was manlier.

The snakes also liked the coolness of the pond but the boys had learned that by hitting the surface of the pond water with a bamboo poles would make a sound that the snakes couldn't stand. Their pre-swimming ritual was to count the number of snakes in the pond, begin hitting the water with bamboo sticks and count the snakes as they made their exodus from the pond. Hesitant snakes were pinned to the ground with a forked stick and their heads cut off their heads mother's kitchen knife. When they came home they carefully washed the kitchen knife and returned it to its place in the kitchen. On occasion the snake count got confused and the boys would spot a snake after they had jumped in the pond. A scramble back to the bamboo and more hitting the waters surface until the pond was snake free and swimming could continue without fear.

Their main concern about getting to the pond, which was located in the middle of the pasture, was avoiding the cows. Scaring the cows away from their water was normally pretty easy until their Uncle Jessie bought a new bull. The bull was a gray Brahma and was very hostile and aggressive. Their first experience with the bull had them fearing for their lives because the bull had came charging after them and they had to run and jump back under the barbed wire fence and dive for cover near a tree that they could climb in case the fence didn't stop the angry bull. They knew that one stumble, slip and they were bull bait. Normally the boys were clothed with only a pair of short pants, no shirt or shoes but they could all climb a tree without restraint. Climbing a tree past the first limb was also forbidden. The bull thought the entire field belonged to him and didn't want anyone or anything in his field. Occasionally the boys Cur dog named goober would challenge the bull but the dog always came out second best and would end up with the boys looking through the fence. A few weeks went by until the boys made a plan. The Red Rider BB guns that they had got for Christmas came in real handy at teaching the bull who is the real King of the field and who the pond belonged to.

Their plan was to make the bull come to the fence and get within close range of the bb guns. Joe was the oldest and fastest so his job was to crawl under the fence and walk into the field until the enraged bull chased him out. Alan and Fred would be waiting by the fence lying down on the ground with guns loaded. Joe would dive under the barbed wire fence between Fred and Alan who were about twenty five feet apart, then they all three would shoot the bull with bb's. The bb guns were not so accurate because the shooting spring threw out the bb in a different direction each time but at the range of four or five feet they were accurate. At first they would shoot the bull on his back legs but the bull didn't seem to mind or he was just too proud to show it. Then after a week or two of ambushing the bull, Fred got an idea; they decided to shoot the bull in his pineapple sized testicles. The results were incredible. Five or six direct hits and the bull put on a good rodeo show. He would buck, snort and slobber but he also backed up from the fence. A couple more weeks of their daily ambushes and Joe being able to get closer to the swimming hole until the bull finally had enough and didn't come charging after them. As the boys eventually walked the 200 yards from the fence to the pond the bull decided to leave them alone and although they had a plan for the bull challenging them as they swam but they never had to use it because the bull had learned his lesson which was "if you chased three little boys and they will make your testicles hurt."

El Toro was tamed and the boys never knew how well their bull behavior modification worked until the day that their father and Uncle had rounded up all the cows and held them in the corral. The cows and the bull were at ease until three little shirtless and shoeless boys climbed up on the corral fence. When El Toro saw their smiling faces he jumped out of the corral and ran to the back of the pasture. Their Uncle and Dad shouted "what's wrong with that crazy bull?" Joe, Alan and Fred just looked at each other and smiled. The swimming hole was secure for another summer and their manhood was safe from their Mothers lye soap baths. It never seemed strange that these three little boys would grow up to become war time soldiers and law enforcement officers who were highly decorated and well respected by their peers. It did seem strange that they lived long enough to grow up.

CHAPTER 17

2015 "YOU HAVE GOT MAIL"

Subject: American ideas

Email of the day
My friend forwarded this to me today with his response.
"THINK THIS GUY HAS IT ALL COVERED. I COULDN'T
SPOT ANYTHING HE LEFT OUT."

Email--

I Am the Democratic, Republican Liberal-Progressive's Worst
Nightmare. I am a White, Conservative, Tax-Paying, American
Veteran, Gun Owning Biker. That's me! I am a Master Mason. I
work hard and long hours with my hands to earn a living.

I believe in God and the freedom of religion, but I don't push it
on others. I ride Harley Davidson Motorcycles, and drive American-
made cars, and I believe in American products and buy them
whenever I can.

I believe the money I make belongs to me and not some liberal
governmental functionary, Democratic or Republican, that wants to
share it with others who don't work!

I'm in touch with my feelings and I like it that way!

I think owning a gun doesn't make you a killer; it makes you a smart American.

I think being a minority does not make you noble or victimized, and does not entitle you to anything. Get over it!

I believe that if you are selling me a Big Mac or any other item, you should do it in English.

I believe there should be no other language option.

I believe everyone has a right to pray to his or her God when and where they want to.

My heroes are Malcolm Forbes, Ronald Reagan, Bill Gates, John Wayne, Babe Ruth, Roy Rogers, and Willie G. Davidson, who makes the awesome Harley Davidson Motorcycles.

I don't hate the rich. I don't pity the poor.

I know wrestling is fake and I don't waste my time watching or arguing about it.

I've never owned a slave, nor was I a slave. I haven't burned any witches or been persecuted by the Turks, and neither have you!

I believe if you don't like the way things are here, go back to where you came from and change your own country!

This is AMERICA ... We like it the way it is and more so the way it was ...so stop trying to change it to look like Russia or China, or some other socialist country!

If you were born here and don't like it ... You are free to move to any Socialist country that will have you I believe it is time to really clean house, starting with the White House, the seat Of our biggest problems.

I want to know which church is it, exactly, where the Reverend Jesse Jackson preaches, where he gets his money, and why he is always part of the problem and not the solution.

Can I get an AMEN on that one?

I also think the cops have the right to pull you over if you're breaking the law, regardless of what color you are, but not just because you happen to ride a bike.

And, no, I don't mind having my face shown on my driver's license. I think it's good. ... And I'm proud that 'God' is written on my money.

I think if you are too stupid to know how a ballot works, I don't want you deciding who should be running the most powerful nation in the world for the next four years.

I dislike those people standing in the intersections trying to sell me stuff or trying to guilt me into making 'donations' to their cause. ... Get a job and do your part to support yourself and Your family!

I believe that it doesn't take a village to raise a child, it takes two parents. ...

I believe 'illegal' is illegal no matter what the lawyers think!

I believe the American flag should be the only one allowed in AMERICA!

If this makes me a BAD American, then yes, I'm a BAD American.

If you are a BAD American too, please forward this to everyone you know ...

We want our country back!

My Country.. ... I hope this offends all illegal aliens.

My great, great, great, great grandfather watched and bled as his friends died in the Revolution & the War of 1812. My great, great, great grandfather watched as his friends died in the Mexican American War. My great, great grandfather watched as his friends & brothers died in the Civil War. My great grandfather watched as his friends died in the Spanish-American War. My grandfather watched as his friends died in WW I. My father watched as his friends died in WW II.

I watched as my friends died in Vietnam, Panama & Desert Storm. My son watched & bled as his friends died in Afghanistan and Iraq. None of them died for the Mexican Flag. Everyone died for the American flag.

Texas high school students raised a Mexican flag on a school flag pole, other students took it down. Guess who was expelled … the students who took it down.

California high school students were sent home on Cinco de Mayo, because they wore T-shirts with the American flag printed on them.

Enough is enough this message needs to be viewed by every American; and every American needs to stand up for America.

We've bent over to appease the America-haters long enough. I'm taking a stand.

I'm standing up because the hundreds of thousands who died fighting in wars for this country, and for the American flag.

If you agree, stand up with me and forward to everyone in your address book!!

And shame on anyone who tries to make this a racist message.

AMERICANS, stop giving away Your RIGHTS!

Let me make this clear! THIS IS MY COUNTRY!

This statement DOES NOT mean I'm against immigration!

YOU ARE WELCOME HERE, IN MY COUNTRY, welcome to come legally:

1. Get a sponsor!
2. Learn the LANGUAGE, as immigrants have in the past!
3. Live by OUR rules!
4. Get a job!
5. Pay YOUR Taxes!
6. No Social Security until you have earned it and Paid for it!
7. NOW find a place to lay your head!

If you don't want to forward this for fear of offending someone, then YOU'RE PART OF THE PROBLEM!

We've gone so far the other way … bent over backwards not to offend anyone.

Only AMERICANS seems to care when American Citizens are being offended!

WAKE UP America

Alan Neil

My Response

I am most of the things this writer says he is but somehow I find some of his beliefs offensive. I don't consider myself affiliated or loyal to any political party but I am loyal to whoever is elected by the majority, when they are in power and I trust them to represent the majority of people. I have never been in touch with my feelings and never tried to be. I live my religion every day of my life. Sometimes I screw up. I like Mexicans because they are not only my country's neighbor they are my neighbors and my friends. Every Texan knows that we had Mexicans fighting inside the Alamo for our freedom. Kind of hard to put in words what I believe or even what I think but without God I am nothing and without Jesus I have no salvation even from myself. My heroes are Lee Marvin, Audie Murphy, Captain Kangaroo, James Meredith, Mohammed Ali, Mickey Mantle, Hank Williams, Nolan Ryan, Joe Louis and that orphaned Mexican kid who grew up in the town just up the road from where I live; The same Mexican kid who became an Army Green Beret and won the Medal of Honor in Viet Nam. It's still kind of hard to say his name. One of my happiest days was when I stood at the graves of Joe Louis and Lee Marvin who are buried beside each other in the Arlington National cemetery. My other heroes were my grandparents, my mother and father, my brothers, my Aunts and Uncles and my cousins.

We all watch wrestling and enjoyed it. If you think wrestling is fake it's because you never wrestled. Most of our childhood me, my brothers and our cousins spent time trying to copy the moves and holds made by wrestlers. I have been banned by my wife from riding a motorcycle because I first learned to ride a dirt bike in the deserts of Saudi Arabia and one year on our vacation she wanted to rent a motorcycle so we could go to the beach. She sat on the back as I drove down the beach the only way I knew how. When the blood returned to her face and fingers I was banned from riding a motorcycle but my memory of gliding over the sand dunes at 100 miles per hour still relaxes me.

My family (both sides) fought in the American Revolution and in each succeeding war. There are streets in New York City and Lubbock, Texas named after my family. The wealthiest town in Alabama was founded by my family after the first born son in America married a Cherokee Indian and the neighbors in the Carolinas didn't approve, so they packed up and moved to the new frontier of Alabama In the War Between the States they fought on both sides, none of them ever owned slaves, nobody made them join the military, they didn't get anything for it and all carried their wounds to their graves. My brother and I fought in Viet Nam and I know the horrors of war but I also know it was a compelling duty that we could not dismiss in any less than honorable fashion. Why we did it was because we knew that all people are created equal in the eyes of God and they dreamed of a place where all people could live in freedom, be represented in government and have the opportunity to become anything they were capable of but live for the good of all mankind. We all offered our life for these beliefs and still we respected the beliefs of others.

I have enough American Native Indian blood in my veins to remind me that most Americans are immigrants and yes there is some resentment within me with the talk of immigration sponsors and following the laws because in my view, they are all revenue enhancements for bureaucrats. I believe that laws of man are a living responsibility of each generation and the laws of God are an eternal responsibility for all generations. No, freedom ain't free; it never has been and it never will be, no one gives you anything free. *If you are free the people who give you something want a piece of your freedom in return. I have never wanted anything that would make me surrendering one ounce of my freedoms given to me by God and my forefathers*

I have lived and worked in socialist and communist countries and they suck at creating people who can dream of a better world to live in, I do agree with the communist view on royalty rule. I don't agree with their views on religion and individualism. I don't agree with socialist views of almost everyone working for the government. Generally they seem to produce lazy people who care less about people who don't work for the government.

When I see a homeless person asking for money, I usually give them some money and talk to them. I know that even though some may have a healthy body you can't see their broken souls or the scars inside them.

I believe that most of the 18th century immigrants to America were products of the European feudal system, or left over's after industries had become redundant or automated and their countries became over populated; either way they were considered property of the owner, they had never known freedom and just being left alone is not real freedom. Some were fugitives from man made laws of their home country. With freedom comes a responsibility most of which they don't see a need for or want to participate in. Simply put they just want to live and let live and expect others to protect their freedom. They can't imagine how one person or a few people can make any difference in defending the human rights of others or providing equal opportunity for all people, they don't believe that humans are God's greatest creation. Slowly the non participants and nonbelievers erode the freedom that my fore fathers fought and died for. Blended into our society are the Africans. Many who came to this country as animals and some were bought and sold like animals. Their forefathers dream was just freedom. Just freedom because before they were sold into slavery they had always lived as free people. Yes I am saying that most of the 18th century white immigrants were the people who grew up in slavery and they failed to understand how hard fought and how important freedom is to all of mankind. The early Africans only dreamed of the freedom their forefathers had enjoyed prior to the colonies of Europe springing up in all parts of Africa, Asia and the Middle East. They enslaved all people for the sake of resources to enrich a proud few so called Royals. Royalty is a word I never understood or do I care to understand. I would rather die than to bow to any man or woman proclaiming themselves as Royals. When I read our Constitution I see loud and clear that our forefathers told King George to get stuffed because we can govern ourselves. Then our forefathers tried to tell us how to make man made laws and how to govern ourselves. They understood that God made laws could not be changed. The one word they got wrong was by saying that "All men are created equal". Had they said that "All people are created equal in the eyes of GOD" it would have stood the test of time because we have spent the next 200 plus years extending rights to people that are not men; Or maybe they should have just said "All of mankind". I have never doubted their intention to do this and I believe their meaning was that all people are created equal and should have the same rights.

Now to put this America melting pot, that I really love, back in order there are a few essential ingredients missing. Respect, dignity, responsibilities to and love of each other; and letting our children and grandchildren grow up with dreams of making the world a better place and to do it without fear.

Differences and Diversity are our greatest strengths. No other country on the face of the Earth can understand this, much less challenge why so many would die for such a simple idea of self governing. There can never be too many Americans. Give us your tired, you're oppressed and we will teach them to dream about a world where all people are free, can govern themselves and have equal opportunity to be anything they can be without injury to others.

Yes I am all the things the writer says he is but I don't agree with any of his views. I suspect that his family hasn't shed nearly as much blood for freedom as mine has. Maybe he did leave out a few things.

Chapter 18

2004 Missing In Action

A military veteran is someone who swore under oath to defend his country from all enemies both foreign and domestic. They knew that this included all things up to and including their life. Most soldiers started in their late teens and few had passed the age of twenty five. The military took them, trained them and made them proficient in killing the enemies. Enemies are defined by the government. Some gave their life and many were wounded but they all knew that old men start wars that young men fight and die in. No soldier wants to give his life but many did give their life not so much as to protect and defend our country but to save the life of another soldier because in the course of being a soldier you become friends of other soldiers. At some point in being a soldier they stop making friends or acknowledging that they are friends because they learn that death cannot be anticipated and except for the grace of GOD that dead soldier could be you. A soldier never forgets another soldier who gave his life to save him. Soldiers learn to depend on other soldiers and they know other soldiers depend on them. Soldiers don't have different skin colors and different languages. This is true even if they are enemy soldiers trying to kill you. Al remembered his intelligence gathering of a dead soldier of the NVA. The only possession he had on his body was a picture of his wife and child.

At that moment he knew that all true soldiers are the same whose intentions are to serve their country and to kill the enemy.

The VA hospitals are where old soldiers go for medical attention for their old battle scars and wounds. Every trip to a VA hospital is a trip back in to the time when they were young active duty soldiers.

Al drove up the old highway to the Houston VA as he usually did every three months. Old age had brought out some new disease from old injuries. He remembered spending three months in a field hospital in Southeast Asia where he refused to be transferred to Japan and then on to the states for better treatment. He refused because he wanted to rejoin his unit as soon as he could walk. Eventually he got his legs working with the help of a pair of crutches and in the middle of the night he went AWOL for the hospital. He made it to the nearest air base for a ride back to the jungle to join his unit. While waiting for a ride back to his unit he met two friends who told him that there was nothing going on at the unit because all air cover had been suspended until our government decided that the war we were fighting was duly authorized. They told him that "we had lost some members and some counterparts because with out air cover all they could do was run and watch from the sidelines". Unfortunately not all make it to the sidelines. Officially they were now listed as Missing in Action. Forty eight years later they are still listed as Missing in Action, but in truth many of them survived but never came home because they saw first hand how politicians caused many of their friends to die. They stayed in the area, got married, started businesses, had children and never forgot their disgust with unpatriotic politicians who got their friends killed. Al remembered his good friend Steve. Steve was one of the most caring people he had ever known but he was one of the missing in action who never came home. They met while working in the Middle East and became friends. Steve was a very health conscious person because he lived in a part of Asia where medical doctors were rare. He married a local girl; they had four children, he spoke the language, practiced local religion and was a keen observer of the local governments. All of his friends were also missing in action and most ended up owning a local business. Steve had grown up in Montgomery Alabama had gone thru the catholic school system and most of his family had served or were serving in the military. He was tempered by the race relations and racism of his early life. He had felt the unjust anger because of his skin color and yet it did not change his belief and love of people. His family had also suffered and when his mother joined Rosa Parks in her protest he felt confused to the hatred reflected on his mother. Steve and Al had talked about the military, growing up in Alabama and politics and had become friends. Al had been living in Montgomery when he had accepted the job in the Middle East and knew the neighborhood that Steve grew up in. The neighborhoods were still segregated so much as the law would tolerate. Rich black kids went to white schools and poor white kids went to black schools but few neighborhoods were integrated. The exception was the neighborhoods around the Air force base where the Air Force War College existed. Al knew most of Montgomery and some things that were truly historic seemed to go completely unnoticed by most residents. Some of the things were the church where Martin Luther King once preached, the old telegraph building where the telegram was sent that declared the start of America's civil war, and the grave of Hank Williams the king of country music, the poet and the man Al had listened to his songs all his life. There were other things of historic value but to Al these were the things that defined Montgomery. The neighborhood that Steve grew up in was near the place where Hank learned to play music from the old black man who taught him and a few blocks from Martin Luther Kings church and close to the main street going up hill to the Capital building where Governor Wallace was still preaching segregation. He had been crippled by an assignation attempt while he ran for President and in his final years he surrounded himself by caretakers who were all black. There was more to Montgomery than met the eye and a complex place for a black man to grow up in but in spite of this Al's friend Steve did not know how to hate anything. Like most overseas workers, Steve was a workaholic and his priorities were a pay check and doing his job better than anyone else. When Steve gave him a package and ask him to give it to his mother Al didn't seemed surprise because it was common to do that for co workers, normally it was some souvenirs of the country they were working in. Steve told Al that his mother would come to his house to pick it up.

In Montgomery Al lived in a white neighborhood near the main shopping mall and when the old Chevy carrying two very black people pulled into his driveway the neighbors gave it their attention. Al knew it was Steve's mom so invited them into the house but she said they were in a hurry; she thanked Al for the package and with out much notice she promptly threw it in the back seat of the car. Al noticed that the driver looked like Steve but without Steve's smile but it didn't make him uncomfortable as he looked Al over and sized him up. Mostly he looked terribly uncomfortable but he didn't speak. Steve's mother said that I have a message that I want you to give my son will you do that. Al agreed and she proceeded to say. "I have four grand children that I have never seen and I want to see them. I want Steve to bring them home so they can grow up like the Americans they are, and I want my son to come home". She hugged and thanked Al for being Steve's friend and slowly got her six foot tall, two hundred and fifty pound body back in to the car and left.

When Al got back to Kuwait he told Steve exactly what his mother had told him to say but prefaced it by telling him "to don't get mad at me" this is what your mother said. Steve started to cry and said "No way have I wanted my kids to grow up in that hatred". Al told him that all of America wasn't like Montgomery and in Houston, Texas just being a Texan meant more than any skin color. Over the next year Steve checked out Houston schools, neighborhoods and local politics until the day he chose Clear Lake as the place he would raise his kids. He got a job in Houston, bought a house in the nicest subdivision, enrolled his kids in school and made it for a few years until he told Al he didn't like working there. By this time his children were totally adapted to America and would never leave for any reason. His children would marry the girl or boy they loved without any skin color considerations and his grandkids were all black, white and Asian. The former missing in action children were firmly entrenched in becoming all they can be and grandpa Steve went back to happily working in the Middle East, practicing his Buddhist religion life style, observing the implosion of the middle east but probably still thinking about the day of 25 years ago when his mother said "I want to see my grandkids".

Al sat in the VA waiting room watching all the causalities of war moving down the halls on their way to below average health care he felt tears coming down his cheeks, not only for his fellow soldiers going down the hall in their scooter chairs, walking on artificial legs, signing their names with artificial hands or being pushed down the halls by a nurse because they couldn't move a single part on their body but also because he remembered the struggles of the "missing in action" and their families. When the nurse asks him if he needed anything for pain he said no. He said no because there was no pain to cause the tears just a wave of love for his fellow soldiers including the missing in actions and the full understanding that they would all do it again just for that precious love of country which is so hard to understand. The love that most government politicians who create "missing in actions" could never understand as well as understanding the life long anger a soldier feels when he sees a fellow soldier die.

CHAPTER 19

THE OBIT

Class reunions are interesting if you have never been to one. My forty-fifth high school reunion was interesting because I had never been to one. After graduating from high school there was two things I was very sure of. The first was I was sick of education and I wanted to leave the small Texas town that I lived in. I had no idea where I would go or what I would but I wanted to work and make money. Years later when I received my 2 bachelor's degrees and a Masters I would think about my not wanting to further my education because it seemed that my education was never ending. The older I got the more I tried to hide the fact that I had a Masters from a distinguished University in England.

Later in my career when I became friends with several business men who were directors of the Foundry in my home town I found it difficult to tell this to anyone my hometown. My father and Uncles and most of my high school friends had spent their entire working lives working for that Foundry. Money earned from that foundry had fed and clothed me, my brothers and my friend's families. Yet there was reason to resent the Foundry because when my father was diagnosed with a career ending condition, he had to sue the foundry to get his pension fund. Disability benefits were out of the question.

Another reason for resentment was the fact that I went to school with the son of the owner of the Foundry and our life styles and week end adventures were much different. My first car was a 1951 Ford that my brother and I towed home from a wrecking yard. We spent hours under the shade tree of our yard rebuilding the car. It took almost a year to get it running, painted and in the process I learned how to rebuild the engine, transmission and literally every thing that moved. We could not afford parts so we made midnight visits to salvage yards to obtain the needed parts. One night me and my little brother stole and carried a transmission for a half mile thru the woods so we could have spare parts. The owner of the wrecking yard was a friend of our father and probably gave us a free pass from arrest. The rewards were great as my first love gave me the kiss of my life in the front seat of that car. The son of the owner of the Foundry flew his own airplane and flew all over the country. He once boasted that President Kennedy's landing in New York was delayed so he could land. In spite of his affluence I felt no ill will towards to him until the day that I got in a fight at school. My opponent was a golden gloves boxer and thought that he could demonstrated his boxing skills on me. My opponent started the fight with his big mouth that his friends seemed to find humor in. After a little wrestling he sucker punched me, we were removed from the school yard, taken to the athletic field house by the football coaches, put on the boxing gloves and told to fight until we had our differences settled. The fight lasted less than 10 seconds because my opponent did not know I was left handed. He didn't know that me, my brother and our friends spent lots of time boxing He started by throwing a lazy left jab at me and I immediately countered with a straight right hand into his face, I wanted him to feel my power and to think that my right hand was my power. As his eyes looked at my right hand I followed up with a left hook to the mouth and the punch drove his lip thru his teeth. We weren't required to use mouth pieces and blood from the cut started as he went to his knees. I followed with another left hook but slower so that I could run the string laces of the boxing gloves thru the cut. Fight ended, coaches called an ambulance and my opponent went to the hospital to stop the bleeding and get stitched up. I went back to the school yard and our class mates were settling up the bets. I saw who bet against me and they were no longer people I wanted to know. The owner of the Foundry's grandson bet against me, he lost. I wouldn't hear his name again until years later when a friend of mine who was one of the Foundry's Directors asks me what I thought of the grandson of the founder. I was a little angered and told him that even though we grew up together, we had completely different life styles, my early life style was reengineering a 1951 Ford and his was flying his own airplane, but I thought he was a dufus. The Director who knew me well smiled and asks why I didn't like him. I told him it was because he bet against me in a fight that I had during high school. He laughed.

The year was 1962 when I finished high school and I was a very confused 17 years old. The town had two main industries. It had paper mill that made newsprint from the regions pine trees and a Foundry that made oil field pumps. They produced top of the line products and provided most of the jobs in the town. There were small businesses in town for life support and specialized in separating the workers from their money. Most people in the town worked where their family worked. I went to work at the Foundry to please my father. I worked in the molding part of the foundry, the place where scrap iron is melted, poured in to sand molds to produce a medal casting that could be machined in to parts for the oil pumps. It was a hot and dirty place to work but working there would forever change me. In the molding department labor was of mixed races but work positions were controlled by the unions. Every worker belonged to a union. The unions controlled the jobs and blacks weren't allowed to become machine operators. They were laborers or helpers, the whites were the operators. I was a helper so I worked with the blacks. The work was hot, dirty and after the first hour of the work shift we were all black from exposure to the molding sand. I didn't understand the segregation rules of separate lunch rooms or separate bath facilities, but because I was pretty much a loner it didn't bother me until one night the operator of our molding machine got sick and the boss told one of the black helpers to operate the machine. He operated the giant machine with skills I had not seen from the sick operator and then I realized that it was only his skin color and the union that prevented him from becoming an operator. The helper and I became friends and he taught me not to worry about right and wrong but to simply be the best at your job and make sure everyone knows you are the best. Then he taught me how to work. Together we sat the production limits and I got lectures from the other workers about not being to produce so much when I got older. I ignored the lectures and listened to my new friend. We had fun working and being the most productive. In my later working life I traveled the earth working in the remote oil patches I always felt pride whenever I saw one of the Foundry's oil pumps. I knew the internal parts of the pump were made by some of my family or some of my friends. They were the best oil pumps in the world and could not be knocked off with cheap copies because every part was perfectly engineered and assembled. My Uncle died during an accident in the assembly plant. He gave his life saving the life of a coworker but still the management delayed his death benefits to his family while they determined that he had been perfectly healthy when he was killed. I remember family struggles when the pay checks stopped and the insurance wasn't paid in a timely manner.

I worked at the foundry until the molding sand started to take its toll on my health and I had my fill of disgruntled workers. I could not see spending my life working there but many of my friends had gotten married after high school, started having children and escape for them would not happen. One day I just didn't come to work and shortly there after the Army sent me a letter telling me to report to and be prepared for. After the army discharged me I spent most of my life working overseas and I had less and less reasons to visit my hometown. During one visit because of a family funeral I notice the old stately mansion of the founder of the foundry for sale. I checked the selling price and my bank accounts and I thought how funny it would be to own the place but I remembered reading a play while I was in Russia called "The Cherry Orchard" and I told myself no way I want to own the mansion. I remembered telling a Russian friend who ask me what I thought of the book/play. I said that I really doubted if any Russian who was born after the communist revolution could possibly understand the story but most Americans would understand it. The old mansion did find a new owner who turned it into a bed and breakfast. The old Mansion was my Cherry Orchard as described by Anton Chekov.

My director friend was an honest man and great at running companies and making money but not all directors are so talented. Most are hired because of their political connections. My friend's years as a director were spent introducing new products and improving sales of existing products. When my friend resigned from the Board he was replaced by another man I had also worked with. The new director was a product of growing up a rich kid who had helped destroy his own family's 150 year old business. He came home from the Ivy League a coke head who didn't fit in anywhere in the company. His father was Chairman of the board and the company sent him to as much rehab as he needed. His first few years of working clean he was shadowed, coached and cleaned up after. I remember him as being timid and vulnerable to the point of not making any decision without advice of the company lawyers. His father finally assigned him to working on a joint venture working with Generous Electric, the best managed company in America. He quietly knowing or not knowing engineered selling his family's 150 year old company to Generous Electric. They broke it into pieces and sold it off in pieces and paid for it all with the employee's pension fund, never giving a thought to the employees or the founders. Eventually a foreigner owned most of the company. When I learned that this man was now a director of the Foundry I knew the end of the Foundry was near. I watched from the news reports, stock reports and family reports as the foundry died.

The last news I learned from the Obits. The grandson of the founder, the kid who bet against me in the high school fight had died. His Obit told the story. In his last few years he had been regulated to being manager of the employee's pension fund. It talked about what a fun loving guy he was and how he enjoyed sharing his good times with friends. His hobby was racing yachts and flying his own airplanes. I thought it so sad that he never had the opportunity to touch one of the Foundry's products in the jungles of Indonesia, the oil patch in Kuwait and feel the same pride that I felt just knowing that some of my family had made most of those parts that were working in perfect unison and how well the final assembly worked in productive harmony constantly producing a stream of life improving revenue for the people, companies and countries.

If my family had spent their lives making Cherry Brandy instead of oil pumps I am sure the brandy would be a priceless treasure for all times.

CHAPTER 20

1998 GREY EYES CRYING IN THE RAIN

The old maps of Sakhalin Russia tell the history of its people. It was originally claimed by Japan, then Russia, and then the northern half claimed by Russia and the southern half claimed by Japan. Today it is claimed entirely by Russia and has been since the end of world war two. The Japanese claimed it as part of their rich fishing grounds, the Russians claimed it as a defense position and then for its soft coal and oil. The second time Sakhalin was claimed by Russia it set up a Penal colony on the Island. The northern end of the Island is near Mother Russia and separated only by the Tartar straights. The faces of the people of Sakhalin show its history and because after world war two the Russians and Japanese sight an peace treaty allowing repartition of all Japanese, unfortunately the thousands of Koreans who had served as colonials in the armies of Japan and they were not included and they remained on the Island. This was probably because of the Korean war and the Russian need for coal miners. They seem to fit in with the Tartars ethnic group from Russia but they were not allowed to return to their homes in Korea. Fifty years after the Korean War ended they would remain in Sakhalin living and working along side of the Russians.

Al knew nothing about Sakhalin Island except flight KAL 007 was shot down nearby and later he would learn that Sakhalin had enough nuclear bombs on the Island to sink it if they all exploded at the same time. None of this mattered when he got the phone call to inquire about him living and working there for the oil company. He had wanted to visit Russia and see these strange communist people who had been the cause of him and his school mates to participate in drills for Nuke war safety. The drill consisted in getting under the class room desk. Even at the tender age of 10 he really didn't think the desk would protect him from nuclear bombs but the teachers took the drills serious and so did Al. His main concern was why they would nuke East Texas, the place he grew up. His understanding of communism was tempered to the conversations of his family when they watched Senator McCarthy exposé" known communist" on the nightly news. It seemed to be horrible that anyone would want to a communist much less that they wanted to spy on America. When the phone call ask me if I was interested in working in Russia, I said yes without asking them any questions about conditions or salary. Two weeks later he had a visa and a airplane ticket. The airplane ticket showed I would go to Alaska, over to Kamchatka, then on to Sakhalin Island. The other passengers on the first flight to Sakhalin were mostly American bear hunters looking to bag a trophy. Al thought them disgusting and compared them to Russians coming to America to hunt the bald eagle.

Three years later he would leave the Island that had enough nuclear bombs to sink all of itself and half of Japan. During these three years he would see first hand the Russian people, the inside of major oil companies, the hearts of people and the one thing he would always remember was the green eyes crying in the rain.

CHAPTER 21

1976 WALDEN'S POND

Al had gone back to see Walden's Pond. He wanted to refocus his life because there had been a few rough patches and he wanted to reflect on his journey forward. He remembered setting and looking into the pond before the army had given him orders to go to Viet Nam. He remembered looking into the pond and wondering if he would ever return; as he stared into those waters and he thought about all the writers and poets who looked into those waters and found the answers and the inspiration they were looking for. He remembered that in 1967 his army company had marched from the nearby town of Concord to Lexington as a tribute for the first American Army's march in 1767. Now 20 years after he got out of the army he was again staring into the magical waters looking for inspiration and answers? His body ached from old war wounds as his mind thought about what he could have, would have and should have done while he was fighting with Post Dramatic Stress and a failed marriage.

The 25 thousand year old pond was well maintained and some improvements had been made since his first visit. The trails around the pond had been improved and along the trails were benches. He turned to walk down the trail when he saw something he couldn't believe. It was Tasha walking around the trail. It had been ten years since he last saw her but she was not one he could forget. When he first met her it was in the Russian Far East. She had been assigned there by the Peace Core but when her job with the Peace core of teaching the Russian doctors English had ended, she had joined the oil company and started teaching Russian to the American oil company employees. Company rules said that all foreign employees should learn the Russian language. Al became a problem for her because he refused to study Russian. At first she thought he was unable to learn but he explained to her that he already spoke Arabic, Bahasa Indonesian and German. He told her that the more proficient he became in a language the more of his heart he lost. In Indonesia his language skills had taken him for an engineering job in the jungles to being an advisor to their Minister of Finance. In spite of attending meetings in 5 star hotels and government offices he much preferred street conversation and cuisine, In Saudi Arabia his language had enabled him to learn Muslim prayers and even though he discovered their prayers and the ones his parents had taught him were not so different but after he witnessed their first hand chopping and head chopping after Friday prayers he concluded that words didn't tell the entire story. In Germany he had listened to old German ladies tell about how World War Two was the most fun time that they ever had in their lives, even if they all admitted losing many family and loved ones to the war. No, he did not want to learn Russian for fear of how the Russian people would affect him as he learned their struggles.

He looked at Tasha and thought about he she had grown as a woman. He already knew that she had transformed herself from a Peace Core worker to a Lawyer and that she had practiced law in her home state of Maine and also in New York. She had told him this in emails but she had not told him how she transformed her body from resembling a Russian bear to the body of a ballerina. They stared into each others eyes and both could see cheek moisture. Al had also had been transformed from a workaholic to an exerciseholic after his doctor told him that cancer can't live in hot blood. After some talk Tasha told him that had she not had twisted her foot they probably would not have seen each other. Neither questioned why they were there. They both thought that just maybe there is some magic in these waters. They sat on a bench and talked and talked and talked. They both knew that somehow in the Russia Far East they had both found strength and purpose to cause them to push until the dreams turned into silent thoughts and the silent thoughts turned into actions and somehow they both ended up at Walden's Pond at the exact same time. Walden's Pond was a long way from Maine and Texas and still further from the Russian Far East or the hotel in Northern Japan where they once spent a week together. He knew that it was impossible for both of them to not think of Japan.

She asks if he could help her to her car and promised him that if he did she would buy him lunch. In one motion he picked her up and placed her on his right shoulder. Her arms wrapped around his neck as she held on and laughed like a school girl. His right arm held her around her waist and they started towards her car. The wooded trail grew smaller and he stopped to lean on a tree and thought that even though her weight wasn't a problem his tiring legs was a problem so he leaned against a tree to balance and give his leg a rest. Then he decided to change the mood from helpless by turning his head and pulling down her jogging pants so he could kiss her stomach. As he kissed her stomach her ticklish surprise turned into passion. She twisted around facing him and put her legs around his neck. She moved up and down as if showing him exactly where she wanted to be kissed. When he found the right spot she started to convulse into spasms of pleasure then slowly began to relax but squeezing him with her entire body. Then she started to slide down his body as if feeling every inch of his body with her body. He became more excited because he could feel Mr. Charlie point upwards and he knew it would be in perfect position to enter her without any help. Somehow she had used her toes to push his pants down to his knees. It seemed an eternity before she slipped far enough down to touch Mr. Charlie and the first touch was overwhelming pleasure, so much so that she climbed up and slid down again and locked them in an embrace of all embraces. Her inner muscles took over as she relaxed her body and she started a rhythmic squeezing from deep inside her that was in perfect beat with Mr. Charlie's attentive expansion and expectations. When the splashdown happened they were face to face kissing so passionately that their teeth were grinding each others and their mouths open grasping for air. Slowly they unlocked and in a moment for eternity they were standing and still kissing. Slowly blood returned to their brain and suddenly her foot felt fine and she could walk. As they walked they talked about his farm life and cows and her father having Parkinson so bad that he required constant care. She would continue to give that care as long as he lived. Then back to New York to practice law and hopefully one day she would become a Judge. He told her that cancer had returned and this one was slow growing but incurable. She drove down M2 to the nearest train station, dropped him off for a train ride to the airport and then drove away with only a smile and a wave good bye, neither one mentioned love, next week or how they felt. They knew there were no words to describe what had happened.

He thought that I really want to visit the baseball hall of fame in Cooperstown but he let it pass and took the train to the airport and waited for his flight back to Texas. On the plane he wondered if anyone at Walden Pond had seen their loss of control but he knew he really didn't care if the entire state had seen them.

CHAPTER 22

1988 THE GREAT ONE

The first Gulf war had started when Iraq invaded Kuwait and tension in Saudi Arabia quickly spread all over Saudi Arabia as the refugees from occupied Kuwait entered Saudi and made their way to Europe. Stories abounded about all the refugees stranded in the dessert to die from heat and hunger. Al knew that the dying refugees would be Palestinians or Indians and not Kuwaitis. American and European soldiers stared arriving in country and the peaceful life style of the Saudi's would be forever changed as the dogs of war came calling. The one of the few jobs outside the oil patch that Al accepted was turning out to be a disaster. He was the deputy director for a large defense project that was installing long range radar stations around the entire country. He traveled to each province and territory of Saudi installing electric generators to power the radar stations. America had sold military airplanes to monitor the security of Saudi and electricity was needed to power the ground stations that would send the information to the command centers responding to the threat. Unfortunately the installations were not complete before Iraq invaded Kuwait. The job was a typical government run job and claim specialist appeared on the scene to determine why the project was running behind schedule and contractors were posturing to protect themselves from claims from other contractors and from liquidation charges from the managing contractor. Every meeting and every communication between contractors was hostile. Al had spent a year driving around Saudi to determine which contractors were tardy in their performance. He stayed in the contractor's camps or local hotels and was always welcomed by all contractors. Saudi was an amazing country and each province was different. In Riyadh there seemed to always be a conversation about women not being able to drive but in the Northern Territory women were not only allowed to drive, they were allowed to operate heavy equipment. He quickly learned that a Saudi woman fully covered from head to toe in black, driving a dump truck always clarified who had the right of way. He also learned that comfort women were available for a price. He learned that in the Empty Quarter he would often be invited to spend the night with a Saudi family rather than stay in a construction camp. Riyadh Saudi Arabia had been the birth place of his youngest daughter but while spending ten plus years in Saudi he had only seen the Royal city of Riyadh or the sands of the oil patch in the Eastern province. The cities of Mecca and Medina were always full of religious pilgrims and the mountain trails from Yemen to Jeddah that started as spice trading trails now contained summer homes for Saudi Royalty because of natures air conditioning, incredible oasis's and mountain views looking across the Red Sea to Africa.

Most of Saudi was completely different to the robust Riyadh or the Eastern Province home to transient oil field workers from all over the world who quickly left the country when the war started because the oil company was trying to eliminate the risk of negligence. A few months after they were evacuated they started to trickle back into the Kingdom when their paychecks stopped. Saudi was forever changed by the invasion of Kuwait by Iraq and Al had only one thing on his mind and that was the safety of his employees. During the first months of the war most European and Americans left the country but the group called third Country Nationals could not leave and the companies did not evacuate them. The country could not function without TCN's. All 45 of Al's employees were Third

Country Nationals and they felt scared and abandoned. He put a plan together for their survival. Large trucks and trailers fully loaded with fuel, water and fuel to be used in the Iraq forces invaded Saudi. The TCN's selection of survival food proved to be a disaster because they quickly learned that without refrigeration bread and goat cheese cannot be stored for more than a few hours and the residual smell of spoiled goat cheese in very hard to remove. In a week or so they were completely sure that they could survive a trip to safety. A team was set up to monitor the news of any Iraqis tanks crossing the border into Saudi. Weeks later when the SCUD missiles were launched the scared TCN's sat of the roof tops of their housing and had a party to watch the SCUD show. Reality set in when one of the SCUDS aimed at the airport hit the housing of American Military and the ammo storage resulting in 30 plus loss of lives. One of the engineers calculated that in one 500th of a second difference the SCUD would have ruined their party. SO they decided to map the spots where the Scuds' hit or were shot down and go collect remaining parts. They fashioned the remaining scud parts into necklaces and bracelets for their loved ones. Fear had turned into due diligence and the night that they caught their assigned news observer asleep while on duty they wanted to hang him. Al stepped in to prevent the lynching for derelict of duty but the message was clear that they had to depend on each other.

Iraq had decided to not invade Saudi but to simply park their tanks in the area between Saudi and Kuwait mapped as the Neutral Zone. The area was home of a large GETTY oil field. It was a piece of land procured by Getty Oil before Kuwait or Saudi became countries and they were identified as British Mandates. Al had been there, spent time there while working in Kuwait because it was near the home of what foreigners working in Kuwait called Diplomat Beach. The beach was protected by large sand dunes and to get to the beach one had to climb over the sand dunes but the reward was worth it. It was an unofficial beach where women could wear string bikinis' and every one has ice cold Diplomatic imported beer.

The crowd was mostly Eastern European who craved sunshine and clean sand. The other beaches in Kuwait were segregated by men or women only. The place was also home to a colony of medium size lizards with purple heads. The war was in a stale mate until General Powell and General Swartzkoff got their people and equipment in place to launch the first Gulf war which would be fast and furious. The parked Iraqi tanks would be killed where they were parked, the US Marines would drive north thru Diplomatic Beach and make it a killing field.

Before the ground war started Al was told by his wife to come home, so he caught the last British Airways flight leaving Saudi. He had never missed a wedding anniversary and this would not be the first. The President of the company was having trouble convincing the directors that Al needed to stay in Saudi. Al told him that when he sent a replacement he would come home. The replacement had arrived and he felt no need to jeopardize the company Presidents support. When the lat airplane left Dhahran and landed in Heathrow he was met by a host of TV and news reporters and the lights and cameras blinded him came on while they interviewed him. The only question he remembered was when they ask him if he thought Iraq would invade Saudi and he promptly answered "No" and then said in Texas Arabic "Sadam mafi lawz" Which means that Sadam doesn't have the balls". Lights turned out and interview ended. Apparently some news reporters spoke enough Arabic to know that you can't say things like that on live British TV.

Anniversary was spent in Vegas as usual, it seemed that time went by too fast. It was time to return to Saudi so a flight on British Airlines was booked. He contacted one of the Engineers to meet him at Heathrow and update him on how the troops were holding on. On a Sunday morning they met at the Hotel coffee shop near Heathrow and the debriefing started. The TCN's were fine and they had learned how to survive a direct SCUD hit if it was carrying nerve gas. The plan was for everyone to jump in the housing compounds pool and cover their heads with rags soaked in some chemicals that would filter nerve gas. It sounded like their plan had a few holes in it but the fact that they were planning survival pleased him.

During the empty coffee shop conversation Al had not noticed the three black men who had sat down next to them but he heard an unmistakable voice. He looked over his shoulder and saw the owner of the voice. It was the American Heavy weight boxing champion Mohammed Ali. The 3 men had distinctly different physical appearances. One was a large bald headed man; one was a small man with a square shaved beard. AS he listened he realized that Mohammed and the square beard were trying to convince the bald head the merits of being a Muslim. The bald head wanted no part of it. Al leaned forward and told the engineer that Mohammed Ali was at the next table. Mohammed heard this and when the engineer leaned over to look Mohammed hid behind a post. The engineer boldly said "do you think I am stupid because I am a Britt, even I know what Mohammed Ali looks like". Al saw Ali smiling. Their conversation about the merits of being a Muslim continued and when their conversation got serious Al told the engineer "not those two, he is the other one". Ali heard this and this time as the engineer turned around to look Ali had leaned forward until their noses were almost touching. The engineer was frozen and the engineer was a Britt of Italian heritage and had a flare for style. While working in Houston he had gotten his ear pierced and his ear ring was a symbol of the Houston Oilers football team. The engineer knew nothing of Ali's history in Houston, him refusing to be drafted by the Army, his great fights in Houston or him being stripped of his Heavy weight title because of what he did in Houston. Ali started having some fun with the Britt. He touched his ear ring and asks what it meant as he smiled at the ear ring. The engineer quickly said he was not gay; it was just a reminder of a football game he saw in Houston. The five started talking about going on to Saudi. Ali and company were going on to Saudi to do some Toyota TV commercials, Al explained they were going back to work on the defense project. They all wished each other the best as they departed.

Some think that every boxing champion is a physical freak of some sort and most of the time it is noticeable but Ali appeared as a perfect physical specimen until Al shook his hand an told him that "I am a Viet Nam veteran but you are my hero because you stood up for what you believe in just as I did" As they shook hands and told each other Thank You Al notices Ali's hands. He first noticed them while watching him try to eat soup. His hand started shaking and he comically slapped his hand and said "I told you to stop it". His hands were shaking from the disease that would eventually kill him. Then the freak questioned was answered. His hands had so much flesh on the back of his hands that it looked like the fingers had been stuck in as an after thought, but Al suspected there was more to the fleshy hands that anyone knew because those were the hands of the champion who fought and beat the best heavy weights in the world. He was not only a champion but a champion with a heart. After fighting Joe Frasier in the Thriller in Manila and the two of them trying to knock each other out for 15 rounds, when the fight was over it was Ali who went alone into Frasier's dressing room to see if he was ok. Al knew that it was unlikely that the world will ever have another champ like Ali. He wasn't just a boxing champ, he was the Greatest One.

CHAPTER 23

JUST ANOTHER JOHN

O n the 4th of July 1970 Al was honorably discharged from the US Army. The discharge center was in Oakland California and it was a busy place. The airplane load of GI's was organized with a group leader and they were told what the separation from active duty would consist of. Mostly getting paper work in order, getting a new uniform to wear home, a uniform that held ribbons for all the medals they had been awarded and of course their last payday including paid time for untaken leave. Before the airplane ride to Oakland they had been told that they may be greeted by war protestors and how to conduct themselves. Al thought of how out of touch the politicians were with the war effort and he reached some peace of mind when he told himself that if he lived long enough there would be an American President, senators and congressmen who understood the things he believed about serving your country and risking your life and limbs for that precious thing called freedom. The Special Operations map showed exactly how politicians' decision and statements got soldiers killed. The final straw was when 3 senators demanded their air cover inside Laos be grounded while they investigated. The mighty Mekong River was a natural border in South East Asia but it was ok to fight on one side but not on the other. Without protective air cover the Chinese moved in and all others fled back to the rivers safety. A few fighter pilots ignored the orders but were quickly grounded or discharged. He had been confined to a field hospital for most of his last 3 months in the Army because he had lost use of one of his legs thanks to a near miss mortar shell. When they tried to ship him home on crutches he ran away from the hospital to join his group along the Mekong River. A few weeks later he was being send home but not walking with crutches. He had lots of pain, no medication but with a heart and head full of pride. His body was pumping enough energy to kill any pain. There were no war protestors at the airport and no protestors at the discharge center. Apparently they were else where celebrating the 4th of July. It all seemed ironic. He kind of looked forward to looking into the eyes of the protestors and listen to their thoughts about the war but he was on a mission, the war was over. He had to get home and figure out how to make a living for a wife and two children. The marriage came after his first leave from the army and the two children were born while he trained and served in Germany. Now the war was over and his life had to move on. He was going home and during the separation from the army he followed ever command of the group leader. The man spoke quietly with conviction and if anyone had comment he quickly drew stares from the group. When they received their new army uniforms he noticed that the group leader had more medals on his chest than any one he had ever seen. He knew that his brother Joe had served three tours in Viet Nam flying helicopter gun ships and he knew that his brother was the most decorated helicopter pilot in the war. He thought of it as if Joe strapped on a helicopter and went hunting just as he went hunting while they were growing up in the woods of east Texas. He had told Al before that he was sick of the war because killing people was too easy but after their cousin was killed on his first month in Viet Nam the war had become very personal for both of them. Things might have been different in their cousin had been with them.

The group leader had a Pennsylvania country boy accent and manners to match. Where and how did he get so many medals?

His medals were not just from the American army but from all the other armies fighting in Viet Nam; Canadian, Australian, Korean and others that he didn't recognize. Al noticed that he had carried a medium size paper bag with him thru the entire processing. He thought that the bag must contain some kind of weapon because he had held it all day long as if were diamonds. Thanks to the group leader the processing went smooth, no talking and except for a lunch break no one had anything to say. At lunch Al sat next to a kid from New Orleans who told Al he was getting a dishonorable discharge in spite of serving two tours in Viet Nam. Al didn't have to ask what part of the Army he had served in because he wore leather cuffs on each arm to cover the burn scars from hot artillery shells. The artillery units were misused in Viet Nam as it became a mobile force to have their big guns air lifted by helicopters and put in a position to kill and protect. Often they were mistakenly dropped inside enemy lines and were over run. Al asks why he was getting a dishonorable discharge and he said that his new commander didn't like him. He told Al that he had not been paid any money and didn't know how to get home to New Orleans. Al had been paid for 4 month of un used leave and without any questions or comments he gave him more than enough money for a bus ride home. Somehow he knew that the kid was a good soldier and had told him the truth.

The walked out the back door of the discharge center to get on busses to go to the airport and Al was the last one out of the building. The group leader had waited at the door for Al to leave. He stopped and opened his mysterious brown paper bag. It contained a pair of jeans and a Hawaiian shirt. He quickly took of his most decorated army uniform and put on the jeans and shirt from his brown bag. He put his army uniform back in the bag and they walked towards the awaiting bus. Then before getting on the bus he stopped by a trash can, paused for a few seconds, looked at Al and put the brown bag in the trash can. No words were spoken. The airplane stopped for onward connections and a 5 hour layover in Las Vegas and Al waited at the gate of the flight to Houston. He got bored and walked around the airport where he spotted the group leader who was setting in a bar and well into drowning his memories. He was smiling and talking to the others as if he was returning from Hawaii … Al thought "if I can live long enough we will have a President who understands soldiers." He had to live a long time. We had Presidents who never served in the military, presidents who were draft dodgers, Presidents who wanted to be soldiers but never were because they had better things to do other than suspend their lives, lift their right hand and swear to protect America from all enemies and it got worse and worse. All the Presidents were willing to use soldiers but they never understood what it means to be a soldier and offer your life to protect our freedom. Some loved soldiers but none of them were soldiers. Finally someone appeared on the scene who did understand soldiers. He had grown up around construction workers and he talked like one; he had success of building projects in some of the hardest political areas in the world. He had been married three or four times but somehow he loved all of his children the same. His father had been a home builder in New York City but his grandfather had ran a bar and whore house in a gold mining town and most important to Al he was a New Yorker. Al never understood why he loved New York City with its oceans of none stop people. He thought of it as walking thru a field infested by fire ants because one wrong step and you will have hundreds stings. Al had walked the streets of New York while he was in the Army, the blocks of streets without a single tree or a blade of grass and he was always amazed how comfortable he felt. He had accepted a job from Exxon in New York City and he had been in their CEO's office. He found nothing to not like in New York city but on the 11th of September he watched TV from his office in Houston as America was attacked and the symbols of New York city came tumbling down as people of fire jumped to their deaths. He watched as 18 year olds joined the military and became soldiers for the expressed purpose of protecting America. He wished he could do the same. Then he watched as the politicians tried to find out who did this and why. I was not a clear picture of who or why. They finally blamed it on a Muslim preacher. They blamed a Muslim preacher. A Muslim preacher that Al had stood outside his mosque in Saudi Arabia and listen to. He didn't preach peace and love, he preached hell fire and brimstone and somehow, some way he got enough money to finance his war against his own misunderstanding of Godless people. Al's own congressman had helped with the financing and giving this mad man preacher weapons to kill the Godless communist but everyone knew it wasn't possible for the preacher to do this without any government help. Governments are all about giving money to causes because they don't work for a living; they get money from imposing taxes on working people and capitalizing resources. Years later the preacher was hunted down, killed and buried at sea but no government would ever be blamed for the death and destruction in New Your city. None of Americas Presidents could even say Muslim terrorist because of a perverted understanding of our freedom of Religion that is guaranteed in our laws. These are the same perversions of our laws that say all men are created equal. It wasn't until a kid that grew in New York City, a man who watched the trade centers fall and finally had enough of politics so that he could no longer live with the fires of unresolved hate. He had a love that politicians talk about, walk around but rarely feel. It seems that this New York kid was "just another John" until against all odds he got elected as President of America.

Printed in the United States
By Bookmasters